Platirius The Rise of
Reve Book II
D.L. Hannah

D.L. HANNAH

ISBN 9781965798003   2024

Contents

To my Isis. The best day of my life was the day I met you.

Chapter 1

Leo Donovan gazed out the expansive window of his hotel suite, overlooking the beautiful waters of Bal Harbour. His inner emotions contradicted a peace seemingly beyond his reach. LesCore Technologies was bleeding red faster than a disemboweled snitch. The culprit? Rubarion Industries.

For five consecutive years, LesCore had been at the helm of manufacturing drugs for weight loss. As the demand for more skyrocketed, billions of dollars poured in, pleasing his investors immensely. Once Rubarion Industries came on the scene, LesCore's stock quickly plummeted.

Frantically, he played every card up his sleeve to turn things around. Although he called in nearly every favor he was owed, nothing changed. There was only one way to get LesCore back on top again. Dr. Revari Ascencio must die.

When all other efforts failed, he'd set his sights on the woman herself. After nearly a year of lavishing her with fancy trips across the seas, expensive jewelry, clothing, and shoes, she rejected his lucrative offer to merge her company with LesCore.

Feigning love, he'd asked for her hand in marriage. She turned him down flat, leaving his ego singed along with his reputation for being the best in his field. He'd underestimated her.

Throughout his life, he thought beautiful women belonged at home, cooking, cleaning, and caring for the family. They had no business running multi-billion-dollar corporations. That responsibility should belong solely to men.

In truth, he hadn't wanted to marry her. While her beauty rivaled most women he'd known, she was much too cold for his liking. She seldom smiled unless she was emasculating him.

Furthermore, she seemed to despise men. When he suggested she step down as a majority shareholder and become a stay at home wife, she'd given him such a tongue-lashing, he never brought up the subject again.

"You're not as attractive as you think you are," she'd coldly informed him. "What commands my attention is money. And power. You used to know how that felt, Leo. Until I tossed the final soil on LesCore and patted it down with the heel of my stiletto."

Incensed, he met her cool gaze.

"I wonder," she continued. "How does it feel to know you've wasted all this time and money on me only to realize the ultimate humiliation of having your investors sell all their shares and invest in Rubarion Industries?"

His enraged expression made her laugh out loud.

"I've been wealthy all my life. Did you really think I'd be impressed by your frivolous efforts? That's what you get for lumping all females together—believing if you toss a few coins at us, we'll drop our panties and birth your brats."

She paused to sip crisp, expensive champagne. "I'm aware I'm a beautiful woman. It doesn't mean I'm stupid enough to fall for your games. And you most definitely are playing a game. One you shouldn't play, as you don't know the rules."

He decided he'd had just about enough of her smug antics.

"Listen, you entitled *whore*! I was running LesCore when you were sampling your mother's tit! It is *you* who doesn't know how the rules work!"

"Resorting to name calling? How chic," she said, tossing an envelope on the table. "Before you put your disrespectful foot in your mouth any further, you might want to peek at that."

She nodded toward the envelope. He snatched it up, ripping off the seal before removing its contents. Beads of sweat formed on his forehead. Thoroughly delighted by his reaction, she smiled as the blood drained from his face.

"Tsk. Leo, Leo, Leo," she purred. "I knew you were hiding something, but I never imagined you were nothing more than a disgusting pedophile. Pedophiles go to prison. And we know how inmates feel about pedos, don't we? If you were cast into prison, they'd clap your cheeks harder than a stripper's...every hour on the hour."

She opened a small mirror, checking for makeup on her perfectly aligned teeth before closing it with a sharp *snap*. "And the guards would look the other way. Money talks—especially in prison."

Struggling to breathe, he watched the maniacal glee in her eyes dance like a majorette.

"You should be ashamed. How old are you? Fifty-eight? Fifty-nine? He's young enough to be your grandson! What is he? Sixteen?"

His jaw clenched. "Eighteen," he said tightly.

"I doubt it," she said softly. "Oh, there's more. Keep looking."

His hands began to shake as he examined numerous photographs of him engaged with—

"My God!" he exclaimed, looking up at her. "Where did you get these?"

Her smile faded. "God?" she asked mockingly, looking around the room. "I don't see any God here. Do you? I obtained them from the same places you did. The Philippines, Ghana, Port-au-Prince, places you thought you could go and unleash your sick sexual desires upon young children. Who would've guessed you're a sick, deranged animal who needs to be exposed for the sins you've committed."

"Revari, please be reasonable! I'll be ruined!"

She scowled at him in disgust. "You'll be ruined?" she echoed. "What about the children whose lives you've wrecked? Do you ever think of the damage you've caused them?"

"Their fathers were compensated fairly—"

He stopped cold at the rage burning in her eyes.

"I've already dealt with the fathers of these children. Putting fathers out of their misery is one of my specialties. No longer will they pimp their children to beasts like you. Now? It's your turn to pay."

"Please," he begged pitifully. "I'll do whatever you want!"

She nodded. "Of course you will. Your first order of business is to sell LesCore to me for a single dollar."

"Have you lost your senses?"

She crossed her legs and made a show of getting comfortable in the plush chair.

"I haven't, but if you don't do as I say, you definitely will."

Taking out a small bottle of lotion, she poured a bit into her palm and moisturized her hands.

"On paper the sale will look like I provided you with a fair price, but we know better, don't we? I'm not giving you a dime for LesCore. I also want your money. All your stocks, bonds, and everything in your offshore accounts."

He observed her nails, then her lips. Red. She wore bright red nail polish and lipstick. Just like his whorish, atrocious mother.

"Can you guess where it's going? To all the young children you've hurt over the years. I can't undo the psychological damage you've caused, but I'll make their lives comfortable. I haven't come to hurt babies. That doesn't serve my purpose."

Confused, he asked, "What are you talking about? What purpose?"

"It's none of your concern." She pulled out a stack of documents from her designer attaché case and placed them in front of him with a pen. "You'll sign these, transferring everything you have to me. Tonight. If I were you, I'd be quick about it. I'm afraid time isn't your friend."

Crossing her arms over her breasts, she said, "If these photos go viral, no one will spit on you. You'll be humiliated and despised all over the world. As you should be."

"Why are you doing this to me?"

"Why not do it to you? Who deserves to be punished more than those who hurt small children?"

Slowly, he picked up the pen.

"Make sure you sign your government name. Not the one you use when you fly to foreign countries to molest children."

Furiously wiping sweat from his brow, he asked, "How do I know you'll keep your word?"

"You don't," she said, her voice cooler than a winter evening in Ohio. "And if you're stupid enough to go to the police...if you tell anyone about our little conversation, you're finished. And you won't get to take the easy way out, either. I'm aware cowards like you often resort to suicide, but that's not an option. Every move you make is being watched and, if necessary, prevented."

Resigned, he placed his signature where required before lowering the pen. She scanned the documents and smiled before placing them inside her bag. Satisfied, she stood, looking down at him.

"Keep the photos. I have plenty more. And video as well. Have a good night, Leo," she said as she opened the door of the luxurious suite he'd booked for them. "And always remember, sharing is caring."

She left him sitting alone with the incriminating photos as he descended into total panic. Now he sat quietly in the dark, contemplating how to get rid of her. She'd misjudged him. He had no intention of ending his life. Hers? Oh yes.

But first, he needed to retrieve the evidence she had on him and destroy the contract she'd forced him to sign. The job he had in mind required only the best. He picked up the phone and called in his last favor. It was his very best weapon against Dr. Revari Ascencio.

While Leo Donovan planned to rid himself of her, Revari was making her own plans. Pressing the buzzer on her desk, she said, "Cyen, come to my office."

"I'll be right there, Dr. Ascencio," said Cyen.

In less than sixty seconds, she was inside her office.

"Yes, ma'am? You wanted to see me?"

"Mmmhmmm," she murmured, looking over their latest stock reports. "We need to hire another influencer to market Allebri. Preferably from the UK."

She leaned back and looked up at Cyen. "Do you have someone in mind?"

"I sure do! Her name is Aimee Lister. She's seventeen and has over fifteen million followers on social media."

Revari raised an imperious brow. "What does she do?"

"She eats while talking about dating."

Revari shook her head. It amazed her how much mediocrity Humans entertained.

"People actually spend their time watching her eat and talk about her social life? God. How many people on this planet don't have lives?"

"It works in our favor. Once hooked on the Allebri, she'll eat like a dog, making more people tune into her videos. I don't think people care about the dating part, but they enjoy watching her eat."

"Why? What's the point of watching someone eat?"

"For some, it's comforting. She's a slim girl, so they don't bully her. If she were overweight, people would watch, but she'd have to have thick skin."

"So, it's pleasurable to watch a thin person eat, yet not as entertaining when a...what do they call it...fat person does it?"

Cyen nodded. "Yes, but Humans watch people of all sizes eat. The only change is the tone of the comments under the posts."

She sucked her teeth in disgust. "That's the most ridiculous thing I've ever heard. Thin people take Allebri to stay thin and enhance their looks. Is this girl pretty?"

"Not even close."

"Then she'll be perfect to make videos about Allebri. Vanity is the window to their souls, Cyen. Get her on a conference call. I'll pitch the deal myself."

"I had a feeling you'd want another influencer. I've already reached out to her. She's waiting to speak with you. When I told her I represented Rubarion Industries, her eyes nearly popped out of their sockets!"

"Excellent! How are her finances?"

"She's broke. The mother raises the children while the father works in some god awful factory. He's an abusive alcoholic, so the girl is desperate to get away."

I know how that feels, thought Revari. "So she'll need the money."

She rubbed her hands in anticipation. "Getting people addicted to Allebri and having them hand in their souls like library cards has been so much fun! Every soul they give empowers my side of Platirius. Once we have enough energy, we'll begin the absorption process."

After freshening her lip gloss, she said, "Pull her up on FaceTime."

Almost immediately, Aimee's face appeared on the screen.

She's been waiting for me.

She gave Aimee her brightest fictitious smile. "Hello, Aimee. I'm Dr. Ascencio, the owner of Rubarion Industries. I've heard quite an earful about you from Cyen. We'd like you to be one of the faces of our new product in the UK. Is this something you'd be interested in?"

"Oh my God, Dr. Ascencio! You're so pretty!"

She laughed. "Thank you, Aimee. You're very kind."

"I'd love to post videos about Allebri. I've heard so many good things about it!"

"Good! I've seen several of your videos."

She hadn't.

"We think you'd be a good candidate to promote our product. I'm willing to pay well for your services." She quoted a figure that made the girl's eyes go so wide they reminded her of the WarCrafts on Platirius.

Aimee couldn't speak. She'd never had her hands on that kind of money in her life. She would be the poster girl for the most popular drug in the world and would have enough money to finally get out of her parents' house. It was too good to be true!

She probed her mind, keeping her smile in check. It amazed her how something as insignificant as money motivated people to do anything. She realized how much she despised teenage girls as she scanned her features—the lank black hair and wide blue eyes. It was probably why they had more girls promoting Allebri than boys.

"Do you accept my offer? If so, you'll need to sign an NDA. As an ambassador for Rubarion Industries, you won't be permitted to discuss anything that goes on in our organization."

"Are you kidding, Dr. Ascencio? Of course I'll do it! Just tell me where to sign!"

While Aimee was acclimating to her new boss's expectations, Allebri's popularity continued to soar. People scrolled through endless videos from influencers raving about it. Social media proved to be the perfect vessel for the drug to reach millions of people willing to sacrifice everything for acceptance and popularity.

The hype surrounding it had swept up Julia Gonzales. In less than two months, she'd lost twenty-two pounds and had no intention to stop taking it. Her favorite influencer, Jia Weston, just posted a new video.

She set her chocolate muffin and milk on the coffee table in front of her before settling in her favorite chair to watch. She smiled and bit into the muffin as the video began.

"Hey guys," said Jia. "I just wanted to hop on here and see how you guys are doing with the Allebri. It's a game changer. I don't know about you, but I couldn't accept how I looked before taking it. It made me embrace myself. After the pandemic, I couldn't fit into any of my favorite clothes!"

She paused to scan the comments.

"It happened to you too?" she asked a commenter. "That's why I like doing these videos. It's so cool to connect with people who feel the same as me. I have more energy now, and I don't have to wear a CPAP anymore. Wanna know the best part? I can eat whatever I want and still look amazing! I'm not gonna lie, when I first started taking it, I was worried about sagging skin and cellulite."

She looked at the comments again. "Yes, you took the words right out of my mouth! Allebri melts cellulite! What other product does that?"

Still monitoring the comments, she said, "Nope! I haven't had weight loss surgery. I took Allebri. That's it! I'm telling you, it works! I've been a big girl my whole life. I know how hard it is when you're fat! I think society as a whole is hard on women. Have you ever listened to these stupid guys on podcasts who claim women have to be a size four, cook, clean, always be ready for sex, and raise the kids? Ridiculous, right?"

More than a few in her comments agreed with her.

"There's so much pressure on women," said Jia, her eyes glowing red. "So much pressure."

Entranced, Julia's eyes glowed red too. "So much pressure," she said.

"So much pressure," repeated Jia.

"So much pressure," her viewers parroted.

I t took nearly three weeks for Aimee to become dependent on Allebri. As an ambassador, she received free supplies of the drug—just enough to have her craving more.

Her videos were a success, receiving millions of views as people all over the world watched the ravenous girl consume large quantities of food. They marveled at how beautiful she'd grown over time and wondered how she managed to stay so thin.

Some accused her of using facial filters for her videos, but the buzz didn't die down. Allebri was selling like wildfire in the UK and other parts of the globe. After hiring Aimee, Rubarion Industries was the number one trending topic for sixteen consecutive weeks. Revari opened a new headquarters in the heart of Edinburgh.

Although she liked Edinburgh, she enjoyed frequenting the cafes in London. She was on her way to meet Cia for lunch when a frenzied Aimee appeared from behind a car. She hadn't surprised her.

Telepathically, she'd sensed her waiting for her in the parking lot, desperate for more Allebri and had made her wait. Now as she noted the wild look in Aimee's eyes, she knew she was ready to give what should've been most precious to her.

To the Human eye, Aimee was gorgeous. Her perfect glowing skin was free of blemishes. Her soft and healthy hair had just a hint of the scent Platirians naturally exuded.

But Revari saw how she truly looked. Aimee was heavily perspiring under a mass of disheveled hair and dark circles under her eyes. Her crusted lips were covered in blisters. The girl was dying.

"Dr. Ascensio," said Aimee. "I'm all out of the Allebri."

Revari knew precisely when she'd run out of product. Gallium made concise doses. No one ever received more than they should've.

"And? What does that have to do with me? We gave you the product to promote and you did. Your job with us is finished."

She started to move around Aimee when she seized her arm in a vise-like grip. She looked down at the offending hand.

"You want to remove your hand or should I break it?" asked Revari softly.

Surprised, she quickly dropped her hand from her arm. What happened to the kind woman who had hired her? She held it up as if her desperation would stop Revari from walking away.

"Dr. Ascencio, please? I feel terrible. My insurance doesn't cover Allebri. It's the only thing that makes me feel good. Please give me more."

Unmoved, she surveyed her. "Then you can buy it like anyone else. What happened to all the money we gave you?"

Tears welled in Aimee's eyes. "I spent it all to get more Allebri."

And she had. In fact, she'd lost everything she acquired working for Rubarion Industries. The fancy loft overlooking the water, the expensive clothes and jewelry, even the new car she bought. In the end, all were hocked to buy more Allebri.

"Well, that sounds like a you problem, kid. We just hired five more British influencers. I have no more use for you."

"I'm begging you. Please give me a chance."

"I already gave you one. How did you repay me? You ended up being a junkie. Look at yourself."

She held up a Platirian mirror to Aimee's face. Horrified by her reflection, she started wailing.

"If I had more Allebri, it would fix this!" she declared. "Please! I need more!"

Now I have you. "What will you give me if I give you more, Aimee?"

"Anything! Anything you want!"

Her desperation excited her. "Will your soul do?"

Startled, Aimee stood still. "What?"

"You heard me. Are you willing to give me your soul for more Allebri?"

She didn't hesitate. "Yes! Take it! It's yours! Just give me more please."

That's music to my ears.

Aimee saw her eyes change from a dazzling gray to a strange bright red. As she gazed into Revari's eyes, transfixed by the peculiar, crimson glow, she heard a range of voices in her head, chanting in a language she could not understand.

She felt worse than she did when she woke up. Suddenly, the voices stopped and her mind cleared. The terrible feeling she'd had for weeks was finally gone.

She handed her a box of Allebri. "This will be enough to last for a while. Call me when you feel better, and we'll get you back on board with making more content for us. We appreciate all your hard work, Aimee."

Sighing with relief, she hugged the box tightly to her chest. "Thank you so much, Dr. Ascencio!"

Revari smiled like a crooked politician. "It's my pleasure, Aimee. You had this coming."

Her joyful smile widened as she stepped off the curb and walked in front of an oncoming bus. She was killed instantly. Revari walked away as a woman screamed. Unbeknownst to

Aimee, she'd swiped the box from her just before she stepped off the curb.

Thanks to the powers she'd inherited from King Barron, the former ruler of Rubarius, no one had seen them together. It looked as if Aimee was waiting by herself before she stepped in front of the bus. Engulfed in the strange red glow only she could see, she collected Aimee's energy and transferred it to Rubarius.

Every soul she claimed produced energy. When she'd collected enough power, Earth would be absorbed into Platirius, making the planet whole again. The feat hadn't been challenging thanks to pathetic people like Aimee Lister.

Her Revaltians were stationed worldwide, collecting energy and transporting it back to their home planet. Chuckling to herself, she walked to her car and started it. Seconds later, a bomb planted underneath it exploded.

L eo Donovan trembled on the floor in fear. Lying next to him was the hitman he hired to kill Dr. Ascencio. His throat had been slashed from ear to ear. With his hands tied behind his back, he lay face down on the floor, grimacing as the hitman's blood pooled around him.

"Did you really think you could kill me that easily, Leo?" asked Revari.

Lifting his head, he saw over a dozen women dressed in red and black gazing down at him with unrestrained hatred. His heartbeat quickened. He moved his face just enough to look at the woman before him. She was impeccably dressed in a red suit and a matching fedora. The heels of her shoes were tall, slim spikes.

She stood and stepped on one side of his head, driving a heel down into his ear. His loud screams echoed throughout the abandoned warehouse. She nodded to Tylo, a Revaltian soldier. When Tylo left the line and stepped on his testicles, he groaned in agony.

Revari smiled down at him. "If you don't want me to cut them off and feed them to you, I suggest you shut up, Leo," she said.

He forced himself to be silent, his heart beating a mile a minute.

"Aww, what's the matter? You look confused." Hunkering down, she asked, "Is there something you'd like to ask me?"

Swallowing hard, he asked, "How...how did you get out? He told me you died in the explosion!"

She nodded toward the dead man. "Who him? Did he lie to you? I'll kill him!"

The women surrounding him burst into laughter.

Revari grinned. Looking up at them, she said, "Well, ladies? Shall we show the man?"

Returning her smile, one by one, they disappeared then reappeared in seconds. He gawked in astonishment before looking up at Revari, who vanished before his eyes.

He flinched as he heard her say, "Does this answer your question?"

Wildly, he searched around the room. *Impossible*! he thought.

"Seeing is believing," she said, materializing before his eyes. "See? I just performed a miracle."

Nervously, he licked his dry lips. "Are you...God?" That earned another round of laughter from Revari and her female clan.

"Oh no. I'm no one's savior." As he watched, her sparkling gray eyes slowly turned red. "Do you know what you signed over to me last night?"

"LesCore," he whispered fiercely. "And all the money in my accounts."

"Oh, you signed over something much more valuable than that. Can you guess what it is?"

He shook his head. "I—I don't know."

"It's two words. Your. Soul."

He blinked. *She wants my soul*?

"So you're the Devil then?"

She chuckled ruefully. "You never tire of insulting me, do you? Now do I look like some idiot who was tossed out of Heaven? Satan looks like you—a male. Everyone knows females are more intelligent than males, especially in other realms."

She plucked a tiny piece of lint from his expensive suit. "Would you like to take a trip, Leo?" she asked suddenly. "I'll put you in first class," she promised.

"Oh yes, please," he begged. "Please forgive me, Dr. Ascencio! I swear I'll leave and never come back!"

"Finally, we agree on something."

An odd chill washed over him as she stared down at him. Fixated on the red light in her eyes, his heartbeat intensified. Terrified, he tried to look away, but couldn't.

A putrid odor of burning flesh filled his nostrils. He screamed again as the light scorched his retinas, sending searing bolts of pain shooting down his spine. As Leo Donovan died, he knew one thing: he would never return.

Generaly Lyric was suspicious. Again. Something was amiss as she surveyed Queen Vivant's portable supper table. She allowed her eyes to scan the spread. Nothing looked out of order. Still, she felt something was wrong.

Her dinner consisted of crispy fillets of fish, cottage-fried potatoes, creamy cabbage slaw, and a side of tiny, spicy dill pickles. Small bowls of tartar sauce, tabasco sauce, and tomato ketchup accompanied the meal.

A thick slice of carrot cake oozing with rich cream cheese frosting and various drinks also waited to be consumed. Her eyes finally swept over a small crystal container.

Gingerly, she picked it up. It was a beautifully designed bottle engraved with delicate symbols. It looked vaguely familiar. She tried to remember where she'd seen the bottle before. Her curiosity piqued, she opened it and sniffed its contents. She held back a sneeze as its spicy aroma filled her nostrils.

It was a very finely ground red powder—not salt or pepper. Shaking a small sample into her palm, she tasted it. It had a bit of heat but wasn't too spicy.

Although she had never seen or consumed it before, she found it quite delectable. The seasoning was the only new addition to the queen's meals. Where had it come from? Grasping the bottle, she called to Sergeant Alicia.

"I'm going to the dining chamber and will return shortly. Keep a close eye on Queen Vivant."

Sergeant Alicia saluted her. "Will do, General Lyric."

A wave of spirited talk buzzed as she entered the dining chamber. Everyone was talking about Queen Vivant's sudden illness. Some wondered if she'd get better. Others feared Queen Revari would be placed in permanent charge of Platineous.

"If Platirius reunites and Queen Revari becomes the only ruler, what will happen to Platineous?" asked Laura Kinley. As the youngest member to join Platineous's dining staff, she was far too young to remember Old Platirius as it was.

"Old Platirius will return," answered the pastry chef, Kate Trawlers, expertly kneading bread dough. "We will be a single planet again instead of two halves. I don't know if I want to see Platirius reunited if it means we'll all be under her leadership. It'll be like having King Dubian back, only in a WomanForm's body."

She placed the dough inside a greased bowl and covered it with a towel to rise. "Of course, I miss my family on Rubarius and would like to see them again, but not enough to be ruled by her! Queen Vivant has been good to us. I'd choose her over Queen Revari any day!"

A few staff murmured agreement.

Cora Coleman, the line chef, poured gravy on a pan of stewed chicken. "Queen Revari has been very generous to Queen Vivant lately. We all saw how she supported her during the DeathCeremony. What an incredible speech she gave. Of course, that's just my opinion."

To General Lyric's dismay, a few more staff voiced approval of Queen Revari. Suddenly, a crisp voice rang out from among them. It was Dora Reese, the chief royal baker.

"One act of kindness doesn't erase all the times that WomanForm has treated us like something beneath the bottom of her high-heeled boots."

She sat a tall chocolate cake on a turntable and began slathering it with thick frosting. "Why, I'd expect even someone as evil as she to show Queen Vivant some form of compassion after her daughters died! Who cares if she gave a fine speech? Queen Revari has been evil since she was a ChildForm. Have you forgotten the treacherous stunt she pulled in her teens? I haven't!"

Carefully, she turned the cake, skillfully filling in the gaps. "Queen Vivant has always shown loyalty to Platirius, while

21

Queen Revari is loyal only to herself! There's no way anyone will convince me she deserves to rule Platirius after all she's done!"

More than a few heads nodded in agreement. All except Laura remembered what Queen Revari did while her father ruled Platirius. While they approved of her kindness toward Queen Vivant, Dora Reese was right—she'd committed an unforgivable act. It must never be forgotten.

Sandi Childler, a prep cook, disagreed. "Queen Revari was too young to understand the ramifications behind her actions," she said sagely. "What WomanForm here hasn't made mistakes in her youth? She'd never been shown an ounce of kindness from her father. I should know—I worked in the nursery chamber back then!"

Placing her hands on her hips, she said, "How could we expect her to grow up as well as Queen Vivant when she's been mistreated all her life? Everyone deserves redemption. Even Queen Revari."

"I made plenty of mistakes as a young WomanForm, but my loyalty to my planet has never been under scrutiny! You sound as if you're more loyal to the throne of Rubarius than Platineous, Sandi Childler!" snapped Dora Reese.

"Queen Vivant is our ruler, not Queen Revari! I wish my poor family were here with us instead of being forced to live under her authority on Rubarius!"

"And that is the issue," Sandi Childler countered passionately. "Whether we live on Platineous or Rubarius, we are *all* Platirians! There is no us versus them, Dora Reese!"

"Oh, no?" asked Dora. "Tell that to Queen Revari! It is she who believes Rubarius is superior to Platineous! Queen Vivant and the Vivacians would be gone *today* if she had her way!"

"Enough," said General Lyric quietly.

Chapter 2

All eyes widened when they realized she'd overheard every word they'd spoken. General Lyric perused each of the WomenForms.

"What you think of Queen Revari is irrelevant. Platineous and Rubarius are still Platirius—two halves of our planet. As loyal servants to Platirius, it is our duty to show respect to the royal family who rules it. Let there be no further bickering among you. Am I understood?"

Guilty eyes darted around the room at each other. "Yes, General Lyric," they said.

"Now," she said, lifting the small crystal bottle. "Who can tell me about this?"

Dora wiped her hands on her apron before reaching out to take the bottle from her. All of the WomenForms gathered around to inspect it. After she poured the contents on the counter, each of them sampled the mysterious powder.

"It's seasoning," said Sandi. "We've served it for quite some time."

"That's why I came to ask about it. It's been served to Queen Vivant, but I don't remember when it was added to the menu."

"It arrived around three months ago," Sandi informed her. "I'm in charge of inventorying all condiments and seasonings." She went to the stockroom and returned with a small canister. She opened the lid, revealing twelve small silver tins. Lifting one out of the box, she said, "This is called CallePepper, but it's not made on Platineous."

A chill coursed through General Lyric. "Where did you get it? From Rubarius's dining chambers?"

Sandi shook her head. "No. Gallium makes it."

The general's eyes narrowed. "Rubarius's chief royal gardener?"

"That's right. He makes all sorts of substances and foodstuffs from plants he grows on Rubarius. About three months ago, he brought a carton and left it in the supply room."

General Lyric found that bit of information very perplexing.

"But years ago, Queen Revari informed Queen Vivant Rubarius wouldn't share food with Platineous. Did she request it? What did he say when he brought it?"

Sandi paused for a moment. "I'm not sure if Queen Vivant wanted it. He informed us the CallePepper was to be served with every meal. He never allows the supply to run out. He always brings more before we reach the last container."

"Does any of the dining staff on Rubarius bring the CallePepper?"

Sandi returned the tin to the canister and closed the lid. "No, he delivers it personally. We've never received food deliveries from Rubarius anyway."

"That's true. He has a high position on Rubarius. He doesn't make food deliveries there, so why does he bring the CallePepper here?"

Sandi removed her apron. It was almost time for the evening shift to arrive. "I don't know. It wasn't my place to question him. I simply accepted the order. But Queen Vivant loves it. She won't eat anything without it."

"Then he brought it specifically for her?"

"No. It is for all of us to enjoy. Everyone on Platineous."

General Lyric sighed. Gallium was a close confidant of Queen Revari. She'd given strict orders she didn't want provisions shared between the halves of Platirius. She found it highly unlikely he'd disobey the wishes of his queen.

Why would he supply Platineous with this particular seasoning? He had to be following Queen Revari's orders. The best way to discover the truth about the CallePepper was to question him.

"That's all I have for now. Thank you for doing a wonderful job for Queen Vivant and Platineous," she said.

"Will she be better soon?" asked Laura.

"I won't lie to you. I don't know when she'll get well, but we must support her and continue serving the throne of Platineous."

She nodded to the dining staff, saying, "In a while."

"In a while," they answered. On Platineous, no one said 'goodbye.' Queen Vivant thought the term was too final.

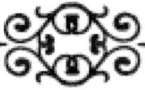

H er mind raced as she returned to Queen Vivant's sprawling bed chamber. After she checked on her, she planned to find Gallium. None of the Vivacians who had eaten the CallePepper had acted strangely. Could it be the cause of her mental decline or had she finally cracked under the strain of losing most of her family?

Captain Kourtney saluted her. "I'm glad you're back. She woke up and said she was hungry."

Queen Vivant was sitting up in bed, smiling warmly at the Vivacians. General Lyric noted the peculiar, vacant look in her eyes remained.

"Where's my CallePepper?" she asked suddenly.

Quietly, General Lyric went to the serving table, pretending to look for it. Discreetly, she slipped the bottle of CallePepper from underneath her sleeve and picked up the remaining sauces.

"Here it is, Queen Vivant. You can't enjoy a fine meal like that without all the trimmings, right?"

"Agreed, General Lyric." She generously covered everything except the carrot cake with it. Savoring a bite of the fish, she groaned in delight. "This is heavenly."

Looking up at her, she asked, "Have you eaten?"

"No, not yet."

"Have some of these," said Queen Vivant, offering a few of the cottage fries.

She hesitated. If the CallePepper was the culprit behind her mysterious illness, she didn't want it to affect her cognitive capabilities as well. In the end, none of it mattered—she couldn't refuse her queen's request.

She sampled a couple of the fries, earning a beaming smile from Queen Vivant. "They're delicious."

She agreed, but thought the food's exceptional flavor was due to the chefs' expert culinary prowess. Although it was unlike anything she'd ever tasted, she found nothing overwhelmingly remarkable.

It had a nice balance of salt and spice. However, it didn't make her crave more of it as Queen Vivant did. She looked forward to questioning Gallium.

The calm energy in the room shifted when General Legend appeared. Contemptuously, she scanned the room before her gaze settled on General Lyric and the Vivacians. She paused to stare directly at Aja, a pretty Vivacian soldier, who returned her stare without flinching.

It was no secret she hated the Vivacians, and the feeling was mutual. The hairs on the back of General Lyric's neck stood up. As the two WomenForms stared each other down, she sensed there was something more to the story than an intense dislike for each other.

In the end, it was Aja who looked away first—a wise choice. Not only did General Legend outrank her, but now that Queen Revari was temporarily in charge of Platineous, she could make her life miserable if she chose to.

While General Lyric still commanded the Vivacian army, there was nothing she could do if Queen Revari decided to punish any Vivacian out of spite.

In a nasty tone, General Legend asked, "She needs all of you in here just to watch her eat? You've been watching too many Human mukbang videos."

"What we watch," said General Lyric coolly, "is our queen. It's our duty. Why are you here?"

"Well, since you report to *me*, my job is to watch *you*," she countered. She gave Queen Vivant a disdainful gaze and said, "Surely you don't think she's feeble-minded enough to choke on her food?"

General Lyric snarled at the petty dig. "You will show her proper respect!"

"Who do you think you are?" asked General Legend. "Let me break it down for you once more. You report to me, not the other way around!"

"I report to you, yes, but that's all I'm required to do—provide you with reports. You're not my commander, nor will you order any of my soldiers around."

General Legend smirked. "Queen Revari now commands you and this army. I'm her second in command. You're not delusional enough to believe you still have the same power you did when Queen Vivant was in her right mind, are you? Change has come. Nothing will be as it was. You best get with the program, or you'll be shipped off this planet on the first craft smoking!"

"I wouldn't be so smug," said General Lyric. "Once she gets better, it's you who'll worry about smoking crafts."

General Legend glared at her. "That sounds like a threat, General Lyric."

"You take it any way you like, General Legend."

"You've always acted so high and mighty. As if you were better than the rest of us, even before Platirius split. But now it's a new day, and a new reign has come. Your queen is crazier than two space cats in heat. There's nothing she can do to protect you from us."

Turning to gaze at Aja again, "I've waited a long time to get rid of all of you. Once you're shipped out of here, I'll sit on the highest peak and watch you ride off into the sun!"

Smiling evilly, she turned to leave. General Lyric's words stopped her cold.

"I hear you enjoy sitting up on high things and riding lately."

A chorus of shocked gasps and mocking chuckles rang out. Aja visibly paled.

Snarling, General Legend turned around to face her. "Just what is it you think you know?"

She met her furious gaze with ease. "I don't think you want to know what I know," she said. "And if I open my mouth and tell what I know, the Vivacians won't be the only ones riding off into the sun, will we?"

"If I were you, I'd be careful about spreading gossip!"

She shook her head slowly. "Oh, it's no gossip. Our surveillance didn't spot the Human sneaking around Platineous, but it caught others prowling around in the dark to break the law."

She stood ramrod straight. Her beautiful face looked as if it were composed of stone. But General Lyric knew better. She had her, and General Legend knew it. Slowly and dramatically, she approached General Legend and stood nose-to-nose with her.

"You're not going to be a problem for me," said General Lyric. "Or I'll become an even bigger problem for you. You may be Queen Revari's *right hand*, but we both know she's cut off the hands, feet, and heads of those who betrayed her. You're nothing special. She has no allegiance to anyone except herself. Maybe you should focus on *your* delusions instead of what goes on in the minds of others."

General Legend's temper flared, but she kept a tight rein on her tongue. If General Lyric knew her secrets, how long would it be before Queen Revari discovered the truth? Something had to be done about her nemesis. And fast. She spun around on a highly polished red boot, quickly exiting the bed chamber.

General Lyric didn't think she'd see her again any time soon. She looked to Queen Vivant, still happily eating her supper. Had she not been mentally incapacitated, the confrontation wouldn't have taken place in her presence. While General Legend and Queen Revari were close allies, she'd been careful to stay off Queen Vivant's radar.

Since Queen Revari had spurned all efforts for reconciliation with her sister, General Lyric suspected Queen Vivant was jealous of the close bond between Queen Revari and the General of the Revaltians.

On the few occasions the Vivacians and Revaltians met with each other, she witnessed the cool glances Queen Vivant tossed at General Legend.

If Queen Vivant discovered what General Lyric knew, General Legend would die—no ifs, ands, or buts about it. She wouldn't be the only one on her hit list. Neither queen tolerated treachery and disloyalty. What she had to do made her heart heavy, but her duty called for absolute loyalty to Platineous.

"Aja," she called. "Come with me."

Startled, Aja looked up as if she'd been in a trance. "Certainly, General Lyric."

She led her out of the bed chamber and into one of the royal gardens where they could speak privately. Pausing to gaze at Aja, she wondered how one of her best soldiers, a promising young WomanForm, could allow herself to be manipulated so easily.

"What was that between you and General Legend just now?"

Her gaze fluttered around nervously. "She doesn't like me."

"Yes, I'm aware of that, but why? Why doesn't she like you?"

Not able to speak, she shifted from foot to foot, silently blinking back tears. She respected General Lyric too much to lie to her, but telling the truth would bring her closer to perilous consequences. General Lyric waited. Suspicion sprouted in her after she'd testified against the Human.

Something one of the justice counselors had said bothered her immensely. Platineous's surveillance team had earned its reputation for being the best at what it did. Before the Human arrived and changed their lives forever, there had been no room for error.

After researching the contents of the main TranScreen's memory, many secrets were revealed to her—secrets she wished hadn't been uncovered.

Her heart sank as the Vivacian hung her head in shame, tears flowing freely down her face.

"General Legend has been copulating with Simonius," said General Lyric firmly. "That is Revaltian business to be handled on Rubarius. But what happens on Platineous is my business. It didn't please me to hear a justice counselor accuse any of my soldiers of breaking one of our most sacred laws."

Aja continued staring at her feet. She couldn't meet her eyes.

"I scanned countless hours of footage to prove her wrong and make her apologize for insulting their honor and mine, but that isn't going to happen. Our technology doesn't lie."

She paused until Aja raised her eyes to meet hers.

"General Legend has never cared for the Vivacians, but lately, she's singled you out for ridicule more than once. She's taken immense pleasure in specifically targeting you. Please don't insult me by attempting to lie to my face. Why does she dislike you?"

She shuddered and wiped the tears from her eyes. "Because I've been copulating with Simonius too," she admitted.

General Lyric shook her head. "You took an oath along with every Vivacian to uphold the laws of Platineous. One of the severest decrees is never to copulate with MaleForms. The penalty isn't just dismissal from the Vivacian army, Aja, it's death!"

Aja flinched.

Her anger rose along with her voice. "You know this! You had everything—a promising position with the Vivacians along with my trust and the trust of our queen! Why would you allow yourself to be drawn astray by a MaleForm?"

"I—I was lonely," she said pitifully.

"Lonely? You have dozens of WomenForms around you. Your Platirian sisters! Ready to fight and die with you in battle! We eat together. Pray together. Laugh and cry together. But you turned to a *MaleForm*? They've oppressed us for millions of years!"

To put distance between them, she began pacing. "They looked at us as nothing more than mindless whores to slake their lustful urges. Queen Vivant and, although I hate to say it, Queen Revari freed us from all that."

The young soldier stood at attention, too terrified to move. She blamed General Legend. Maybe if she hadn't been so blatantly petty, her relationship with Simonius wouldn't have been discovered.

"But you turned your back on all she's built. You've thrown away not only your career, but your *life* to betray your queen! Can you explain that, soldier?"

She shook her head sadly. "No...but he made me feel beautiful."

"Beautiful? You're a member of the greatest army under the greatest queen in the universe. She made history as the first WomanForm to rule Platineous. Planets are ruled by MaleForms throughout the galaxy. Some were sent back in shame and defeat after they waged wars to dethrone her."

Aja wiped her tears as she continued tearing into her.

"You have the gall to stand there and tell me you pissed away your future because a MaleForm fed you a compliment? Do you realize he only said it so you'd lie with him? He's been copulating with General Legend too."

She wanted to roll her eyes but didn't. If it was true, then General Legend had forced him to. She wasn't his type. She trusted Simonius. No one would turn her against him.

General Lyric knew exactly how he operated, but trying to convince her was pointless. She'd already gone too far. "How beautiful were you to him as he lay on top of her? You were beautiful when you fought gallantly in your queen's army. You were beautiful when you defended Platineous against our enemies. There's nothing beautiful about betraying your queen for a sneaky MaleForm!"

Aja began crying harder but the general wasn't moved.

"Queen Vivant isn't well enough to lead us now, but I'm still commander of the Vivacians. I cannot and will not overlook what you've done. You will tell me the truth. Are there more who have copulated with Simonius? Is there anyone else who knew what you were doing with him? Don't hesitate, and don't get quiet, soldier. My patience with you has just about exhausted."

"As far as I know, I'm the only Vivacian he's been with. But I've heard he's copulated with many Revaltian soldiers."

General Lyric nodded solemnly. "That's for Queen Revari to handle then."

"I've never told any of my teammates what I did with him. We thought we were being careful."

"Clearly you weren't careful enough if the justice counselor knew. How did she find out?"

"She caught us in one of the gardens. She was in the process of drafting a report for Queen Vivant. She intended to give it to her after the princesses' Life Celebration. Then the princesses died and Queen Vivant became ill."

She sniffed. "She hates Queen Revari for sending one of her daughters to the Chamber of Despair, so I doubt she'll report it to her. I believe she's waiting for her to get better. Queen Vivant is the only one with the authority to punish me."

General Lyric stopped pacing and got in her face. "Are you being passive-aggressive?"

Dry-eyed now, Aja's insolent stare infuriated her. "Well, it's true. As long as she's ill, I won't get into trouble."

A wave of panic rushed through her. "What do you know about her illness? Did you have anything to do with the murders of the princesses or her losing her sanity?!"

"By the Heavens, no! I would never hurt Queen Vivant or her daughters! It sounds terrible, but the tragedies worked out in my favor! I fear for my life! I don't want to die!"

She wondered how she could've misjudged her. In many ways, she reminded her of Queen Revari—mean-spirited and selfish. She wasn't fit to serve in the Vivacian army.

"Had you been more careful to keep your eyes on your future instead of what was between Simonius's thighs, you wouldn't be in this position," she said. "Allow me to assist with your lack of clarity on how things operate on Platineous. As general, I may not be able to punish you for what you've done. However, I am well within my authority to have you locked up."

Aja's confident demeanor deflated like a balloon.

"You're wrong in assessing Queen Vivant's capabilities, soldier. Queen Revari is in charge. Your punishment will come from her, not Queen Vivant."

Her knees buckled. "Oh no! Not her! You're not going to report me to Queen Revari, right? Please, General Lyric, I don't want to die!"

"You knew the rules of the game before you broke them," she said sternly. "Although it's clear General Legend already knows about you and Simonius, I'll have to make a formal report to her. It doesn't matter what the justice counselor does."

General Lyric's gaze was cooler than ice. "My loyalty is to Platineous. Had you shared the same notion, this wouldn't be happening now." Pivoting her head towards a tall bunch of shrubs, she said, "Vivacians."

Immediately, three Vivacian soldiers appeared. "Yes, General Lyric."

"Take Aja to the confinement chamber and lock her up. As of now, she is immediately discharged from the Vivacians."

Nodding to them, she turned her back on Aja and headed for Rubarius. She had no power to lock up MaleForms on either side. Neither did General Legend. Only the queens had the authority to punish them. She knew what would happen to Simonius once Queen Revari discovered his treachery.

But she wondered what she'd do to General Legend, who had served her long before she ascended to the throne of Rubarius. One would even say they were friends. Still, Queen Revari valued loyalty over friendship. She suspected General Legend's time was ending faster than she imagined.

To her credit, she pretended to be surprised to learn about Aja and Simonius. "So she's locked away in your confinement chamber? Good work. Don't worry about telling Queen Revari anything. That's my job."

General Lyric knew she had no intention of telling Queen Revari about Aja and Simonius. Queen Revari was exceptionally intelligent—and merciless. Upon discovering what he'd done, she'd have him tortured before execution.

That meant he'd expose every WomanForm he'd copulated with, including General Legend. No—she'd try to keep this from Queen Revari for as long as possible.

She thought that would only make matters worse. Discovering her second in command had broken one of her most sacred laws was one thing. It was quite another to know she'd intentionally kept secrets from her. One might wonder what other secrets General Legend withheld from Queen Revari.

In the end, it was her business. If she wanted to extend the rope to hang herself, then General Lyric was all for it. Now she needed to meet with Gallium about the mysterious CallePepper.

S he found Gallium to be more forthcoming than General Legend. He didn't beat around the bush or attempt to hide his dislike of her—and Queen Vivant.

"You crossed over here from Platineous to ask me about seasoning?" he asked scornfully. "Shouldn't you be looking after your queen?"

"I'm aware of my duties, Gallium. I don't need you to remind me what I've been sworn to do."

"Good for you. I'm aware of my duties too. I'm also aware I don't report to Vivacians. Only Queen Revari has the right to question me about anything that transpires in Rubarius and now—Platineous. Therefore, I can't help you."

"I merely asked why you brought the CallePepper to Platineous when Queen Revari ordered food not to be shared among the two realms."

He pulled a sizeable green plant from a jardiniere, slicing it with the precision of a surgeon.

"Have you ever heard of one changing their mind? Surely, one may freely do so without being subjected to asinine questions?"

He was everything she detested about MaleForms. Arrogant. Disrespectful. Dismissive.

"Platineous doesn't receive any supplies except the CallePepper. You don't find that strange?"

"No stranger than you standing here questioning me as if I'm one of your Vivacians," he retorted. "You act as if there's some dark mystery surrounding Queen Revari being generous when that's all it is—generosity. When she sampled it, she liked it. We had more than enough, so she told me to provide Platineous with it so we didn't have an overflow."

She watched as he placed the plant inside a machine to extract its juice.

"That's it. She's not the monster you paint her to be. I'll admit she doesn't show it often, but she has a heart. There's no reason to go off half-cocked like some demented detective bent on finding deception in everything she does."

While he sounded reasonable, his body language betrayed his rational tone. He was tense, she noted. Guarded. If there was nothing suspicious about the CallePepper, he would've been more relaxed. He watched her just as closely as she watched him.

"If you're so curious about the CallePepper," he said slowly, "why don't you ask Queen Revari about it once she returns?"

Although she kept her face devoid of emotion, he smiled. "But we both know you won't. If there's nothing else, I have work to do."

"I'll let you get to it then."

"Yes please," he said tersely. "Oh, and...please give my regards to Queen Vivant. I hear she's just turned seventeen. She's growing up so fast!" His cruel laugh echoed inside the gardening chamber.

Appalled by his flagrant scorn, she snapped, "How dare you disrespect our queen!"

He quieted, undaunted by her indignant outrage. "She's your queen, not mine," he said icily. "My queen is entirely in charge of her mind...and her planet. You'd better get used to it."

"That's the second time I've been told that by a Revaltian."

"I'm no Revaltian." His eyes were colder than the sea on an early winter morning. "And I have no issue correcting you until you finally learn who is in control. It is Queen Revari. It's her time now, and nothing you say or do will stop her from fulfilling her destiny."

"It is Queen Vivant who corrects me."

"Queen Vivant can't correctly avoid coloring outside the lines in a coloring book. It must be tough seeing your queen act like a toddler, but again, you should get used to it. This is your new reality." He mixed various powders into the juice until he formed a paste and sat it under a special lamp to dry.

"Once the justice council realizes this and permanently appoints Queen Revari as the leader of a united Platirius, she can put your queen out of her misery and get rid of you and the rest of Vivacians. Then we all can return to living our lives under one authority. The true ruler of our planet—Queen Revari."

"You're so confident we're just going to fade away. You're not a bit heartbroken over the loss of the princesses. It's as if you were waiting for all this madness to happen."

"The only madness I see is standing right in front of me. I'm not obligated to display any emotion in front of you. If you don't stop with all these—conspiracy theories—the council may usurp you from your duties as general and lock you away in a room next to a drooling Queen Vivant. You sound just as crazy as she is."

She could hear no more. She turned and left him sitting among the noxious roots of his plants...and his venomous tongue.

Chapter 3

In another time and place, Revari was in an excellent mood. Leo had been so caught off guard by the blackmail, he hadn't realized she wasn't interested in acquiring LesCore. She wanted access to all his liquified assets. She transferred the funds into Dellah Peterson's offshore accounts.

'Dellah Peterson' had no traceable connection to him or LesCore. True to her word, she distributed the funds equally among his victims and released the damaging photos and video to the media. Once the public caught wind of his predatory nature, the once revered reputation of LesCore disappeared like a puff of smoke.

The police found him swinging from a light fixture in one of the master bathrooms of his mansion. His death was ruled a suicide. She couldn't have planned it more perfectly.

Humming softly, she pulled a pan of enchiladas out of the oven. The hot, bubbly cheese glistened as she set the pan on the counter beside piquant gazpacho, a dish of platanos maduros, and succulent Spanish rice to cool. She intended to have a nice supper and read some reports before bed.

She set two places as she'd done more years than she wanted to remember and lit three tall, creamy candles. The blue and white china dishware and expensive cutlery sparkled under the soft lighting. She stood back, admiring the beautiful table she'd set. It was missing something.

Smiling, she unwrapped a bouquet of white roses, hydrangeas, and lilies she'd purchased. She placed the flowers in a crystal vase and sat them in the middle of the table. Now the table was perfect. She served up the food, opened an expensive bottle of wine, and sat down to eat.

Everything was going perfectly. She felt no need to check on how things were going on Platirius. Over the years, General Legend had proven she could lead in her absence. Her focus would remain on Earth until she accomplished what she set out to do.

She took a bite of the enchiladas, savoring their rich, spicy flavor. It had been the first dish Oliver taught her to make. She immersed herself in his culture during their short time together. After the Ascencios enrolled her in school, she excelled as a gifted student.

The following year, she earned her high school diploma and an associate degree in an accelerated program. She wanted to be a first-grade teacher while Oliver made a comfortable living as the CEO of Blind Trust. Blind Trust made software for people with visual impairment.

They lived a quiet and peaceful life after they married in a small, intimate ceremony. After Oliver made The World's Most

Powerful People with Disabilities list, they went on a second honeymoon. She never realized she could be so happy. She hadn't missed living on Platirius. In fact, she found it easy to forget all the misery she'd left behind.

She'd been getting ready for class when she felt a strange fluttering in her belly. Confused, she'd gone to Oliver's mother and told her about feeling queasy in the mornings. With a secretive smile, she scheduled an appointment for her. In less than a week, she discovered she'd be a mother.

She could barely contain her excitement when she surprised Oliver with the news. She hadn't expected him to cry and became alarmed, thinking he didn't want their child. But he pulled her close, hugging her tightly. She hugged him tighter, relieved he wouldn't abandon her and their child.

Oliver was overjoyed to learn she was pregnant. Many nights after she'd fallen asleep, he held her close to his heart, terrified he'd awaken one morning to discover she'd returned to Platirius.

Although stories about her home planet were often sad, he visualized the luxurious lifestyle she'd been born into. He worked hard to provide her with the best money could buy.

He never wanted her to look at him and find him lacking. She was a beautiful woman who had her choice of any male on either planet. He'd surely die of a broken heart if she left him.

On the contrary, she had no intention of returning to the hell she'd escaped from. She doubted King Dubian or Princess Vivant missed her. She missed her sister, but it wasn't enough to give up the wonderful life she'd built with the man she loved. Now...she would be bringing a new life into existence.

She intended to be the best wife and mother she could possibly be. She was married to a man she loved—not a stranger King Dubian chose for her.

Everything was going perfectly until Princess Vivant found her. At first, she tried to ignore the mental probing she felt. She had no interest in speaking to her. However, as the telepathic connection they shared became more intrusive, waking her up in cold sweats, she knew she had to answer.

She waited until Oliver went golfing with his father before she finally granted her access. Concentrating hard, she allowed her to materialize in front of her. While Princess Vivant was overjoyed to see her, she didn't return her enthusiasm.

"Princess Revari! By the Heavens, where have you been? Father has had the Platirian army searching the entire galaxy for you!" She scanned her carefully. "You look so...plain. Are you all right? Have you been kidnapped?"

Revari frowned at her. "Of course not. As you can see, I'm fine. Although you say I look plain, I'm the happiest I've ever been."

She looked around the neat, modest bedroom. "But how? You're living on Earth. You're away from your home and your family. This is half the size of one of your bedroom closets. You can't possibly be happy here."

"Who are you to tell me what should and should not make me happy?" snapped Revari. "You've had everything spoon-fed to you all your life! Shouldn't you be concentrating on your own husband?"

She stared at her. "Please don't tell me you married a...Human?!"

"What if I did? And what is it to you? I have a good life here and I'm happy. Shouldn't that be enough for you? Or do you miss seeing me miserable?"

She dodged Princess Vivant's outstretched hand.

"That's not true. I've never enjoyed seeing you unhappy! You have to give Father a bit more time—"

Reaching her breaking point with her, she exploded. "I don't need to give King Dubian a blasted thing! I have a father who treats me like his own daughter. For the first time, I know what it means to be loved. To be wanted and treated as a member of a family."

Princess Vivant's haughty gaze was eerily similar to King Dubian's. "No Humans could ever be your family. We are Platirians. We're above Humans. Do you hear what you're saying? You don't sound well!"

"I'm perfectly healthy. The only time I've been sick was when I lived on Platirius. I was sick to death of your cruel brute of a father and your arrogant husband acting as if they alone were the sun and the moon. That life might be sufficient for you, but it isn't for me! Not anymore. I'm never returning to Platirius."

She gaped at her. "You don't mean that. Surely you don't mean what you're saying."

She wanted her sister to leave. Immediately. "I mean precisely what I say. You're just as arrogant as King Dubian. I know he had you probe my mind to find out where I was."

"Of course he did, and I was happy to do it. Father misses you!"

She waved a dismissive hand in the air. "Oh, stop lying. Do you hear what you're saying? He despises me. He misses humiliating me in front of everyone by parading you around like a prized pony so everyone can see how you're his beloved daughter and I'm the murderer who killed his wife! You're blind. You've always chosen to be blind to who he is."

She turned away as Princess Vivant caught her arm. "I can see much clearer than your Human."

Revari stilled at her soft, impertinent tone. "You haven't just found me. You've known all along I was here, didn't you?"

Her voice rose when she remained silent. "Didn't you?"

"We've always been connected. Of course I knew where you were. I've seen everything. When you crashed the craft and met the Human, I could smell his strange scent. Humans smell like space hounds. I can't believe you live among them without gagging."

"The only one who makes me want to gag is you. You can leave. We're finished. Today. Forever."

"But Father wants you to come home!"

"Does it look like I care what he wants? I've already told you my family is here. I'm not returning to Platirius."

She looked at her as if she'd grown two heads. "You've lost your mind."

"No, I've found myself. I've discovered I am worthy to be loved and supported. I don't have to accept being treated like trash. I don't expect you to understand that. Just go. Go and never come back."

Platirians had always compared her to King Dubian, but now Revari realized her sister had more of his ways than she had imagined.

"Now that I know you've been secretly spying on me, I'll make sure you never probe my mind again. You're just as awful as your father. Perhaps more."

"I'm your sister. I know things have been tough between you and Father, but I want what's best for you. I've convinced Father to allow me to choose a husband for you instead of him."

Revari scoffed. "Corporal Fontine?"

"Don't be silly. He's a commoner. The MaleForm I've selected is Colonel DaCosta. He's a fine soldier and has earned the complete trust of Father and General Kron. He'll make a wonderful husband for you."

She stared at her. She wasn't surprised her sister didn't respect the boundaries she had set. Their father had reared her to believe she was superior to her. "Your arrogance knows no bounds. Have you not heard a word I said? I'm already married! I love my husband, and...I'm carrying his child! There is nothing you can say to make me give up the life I have here."

She stared at her in horror. "You're jesting! Please tell me you haven't given your virginity to a Human? And carrying an abomination?!"

Revari slapped her across the face. Hard. "If you ever insult my baby again," she said through clenched teeth, "I'll kill you!"

She touched her stinging cheek, her eyes wide with shock. Although she'd occasionally been angry with her, her sister had never hit her. Never.

Revari glared at her. "It's time to go." she said, raising her hand.

"No! Sister, please wait!"

It's too late, she thought as she teleported her home. *It's much too late for you to act like a sister now.*

She didn't know how or when her powers had grown more substantial than her sister's, nor did she care. She was done with Platirius.

As Princess Vivant materialized in King Dubian's meeting chamber, General Kron ran to her with the king following close behind.

"What happened? Did you see her?" asked King Dubian frantically.

"Yes, I found her," said Princess Vivant softly. "She said she's not coming back."

Someone gasped behind him. He whirled around in a huff, daring anyone to say something.

"She doesn't get to decide where she lives!" he said. "And on Earth, of all places!"

"Father, she married a Human. And she's carrying his InfantForm."

His eyes narrowed. "What did you just say?"

General Kron spied a mass of red welts materializing on her pretty face. Using great care, he tilted it towards him. "What happened to your face?" he asked.

"She hit me. It was my fault. I called her InfantForm an abomination."

"That's precisely what it is!" said King Dubian. "What was she thinking?"

General Kron gently caressed her cheek. "It doesn't matter what you said. She had no right to strike you."

"The little brat! I'll have her dragged back here! Does she realize the embarrassment she's caused? She's betrayed her planet for a mere Human! She's brought shame to me! On her mother's memory! She'll be severely punished!"

"Father! You promised if I connected with her, you'd be kind to her! She ran away because she was unhappy! How will she trust us again if you continue making her feel unloved?"

"ChildForm! Do you realize what your sister has done? She's committed treason! I cannot allow that to stand! I'd be the laughingstock of every planet!"

"I would think your daughter would be more important than your reputation. Princess Revari is living among Humans because she feels like a foreigner among her race."

His jaw clenched.

"She was so distraught that she turned to a Human. Punishment isn't a solution. We must help her see reason and return home."

She grabbed her husband's hand. "I'm going to my bed chamber to lie down. When I wake up, I hope we'll have an amicable solution for how to guide her home." She planted a soft kiss on his cheek before turning to King Dubian. "I'll see you in a while, Father."

Oh yes, thought King Dubian. He had a solution to the problem. One Princess Revari would never forget.

Revari waited until Oliver came home to tell him what happened. "It's not safe here anymore, Oliver. We have to hide somewhere my father can't find us."

"You say your sister is telepathically connected to you. Where would we go they couldn't find us?"

"I blocked her powers from tracking me. There's no way King Dubian can find me without her." Observing his worried expression, she asked, "Do you trust me?"

He grabbed her hands. "You know I do. Just tell me what to do, and it'll be done." He quickly called his parents and told them what happened.

"You have no choice then. You can't allow him to take your wife back to that awful place," said Mr. Ascencio. Her in-laws had never questioned her story of coming from another planet. They loved her just as fiercely as they loved their son. To them, she was family, and families protected each other.

"Your uncle has a villa in Cuba," he said, placing two passports in Revari's hands. "I've already made the arrangements. You'll be safe there."

Mrs. Ascencio couldn't stop crying. "Promise you'll call us when you arrive and tell us you made it safely?"

"Of course, Mami. I promise," said Oliver. Tearfully, they said their goodbyes and placed their luggage in the back of Oliver's Range Rover.

"Revari, if you get tired before you reach the airport, pull over at a rest stop. Don't put unnecessary strain on you and the baby."

"Okay, I will. We'll call soon. Don't worry." she said, kissing her cheek. The Ascencios had been one of the blessings she had prayed for. She hoped they'd see them again soon.

She knew she didn't need rest. She didn't tire as quickly as Humans. She drove to the airport and Oliver called his parents just before they boarded the plane.

"Mami, please don't cry. This is only temporary. Yes, you'll be holding your grandchild in your arms very soon. We have to be sure Revari and the baby will be safe."

"Promise me," said Mrs. Ascenscio. "Promise me we'll all be together again, Oliver."

"I promise. Nothing will keep us apart."

They arrived in Cuba and traveled to his uncle's villa in style. The Ascencio family was very wealthy. Oliver's uncle had spared no expense to accommodate his only nephew. They bought fresh produce from local vendors and shopped at expensive boutiques.

Loaded with bags of fashionable maternity clothes, baby toys, and delicious delicacies, they returned to the villa to eat a lavish meal prepared by a chef before finally lying down in the beautifully decorated master bedroom.

At daybreak, she rolled over and tried to snuggle closer to her husband. When she reached for him, she felt nothing. Alarmed, her eyes snapped open to find him kneeling between two Platirian soldiers.

King Dubian's soulless eyes penetrated hers. "Hello, my daughter."

It was the last thing she remembered.

The days and nights wove together. She had no idea how long she'd been kept in the confinement chamber. During the brief periods she was allowed to shower and eat, she planned how to find Oliver. She cursed herself for letting Princess Vivant speak with her.

She knew how King Dubian operated. By running away from Platirius, she'd humiliated him and hurt his pride. He was far too vengeful to let it pass without exacting revenge.

Oliver was no match for him. He'd kill him just to get back at her. She had to find her husband and leave Platirius. Before she could think of a way, the door opened.

She steeled herself, ready to give whoever entered a tongue lashing they wouldn't forget. It was Princess Vivant.

"It was you who told him where I was, wasn't it?" asked Princess Revari. "How could you possibly find me without the telepathic link?"

"I used your *nued points*," said Princess Vivant.

On Platirius, *nued points* were points of origin within the body that could be tracked with Platirian technology. Scanners virtually removed clothing to gain access to them.

Once in sync, they gave off vibrations, acting like a homing device that led straight to the missing target. Every Being had *nued points*, but Humans were not sophisticated enough to know how to use them to find missing people on Earth.

Her stomach rolled. It didn't surprise her that her father had spared her no decency. And her sister had gone along with it.

Princess Vivant watched her fury rise. "Don't look at this as bad. You're home now. You can return to living the life of a princess instead of a lowly Human. Things will return to normal once Father decides what to do with the...half InfantForm."

"He won't touch my baby!"

"I understand you're upset, but in time, you'll understand why I felt it was necessary to return you to Platirius."

She tried to touch Princess Revari's hair, but dropped her hand as she shook her head violently.

"Once Father discovered you were gone, he ranted and raved, but didn't want you to be found. I convinced him to find you and bring you back home."

"What?! How could you do such a thing?!"

"Here is where you belong. You're a Platirian, not a Human! Once you've spent time in the Chamber of Despair, getting the help you need, you'll begin to see things more clearly."

"Are you out of your mind, Vivant? No one is locking me away with weak-minded Platirians!"

"Isn't that what the Humans have done to you? Weakened your mind? You're not the fearless sister I remember. You used to know who our enemies were." Her beautiful face was clouded with contempt. "You've placed them above your kind. You've changed."

Princess Revari stared at her in amazement. "You're not my mother. It isn't your place to control my life!"

"Someone has to. You've lost control of yourself. That half InfantForm is the last connection you have to the Humans. Once Father decides what to do with it—"

"YOU'RE NOT TOUCHING MY BABY!!" she screamed, panting wildly.

The imminent threat to her child, coupled with the long days and nights in captivity, finally took its toll on her. She struggled against the bonds, attempting to free herself.

"I WILL KILL YOU, VIVANT!! DO YOU HEAR ME?? IF YOU LAY ONE FINGER ON MY BABY OR OLIVER, YOU'LL DIE!!"

"You don't realize how far you're gone. I never said I or Father would harm it."

"What do you think he's going to do with it, you fool?! Enlist it in his army?! It's half-Human! He'll never allow it to live!"

"You're being too harsh about Father. Give him a chance to make things right. I'm carrying as well. Father was overjoyed to hear General Kron and I were expecting. I wanted you here to be an aunt to my baby. I like the sound of that—"

Princess Revari spit in her face. Startled, Princess Vivant wiped the offending blob from her cheek with her scarf.

"Do you see what I mean? You've gone mad."

She spat on her again. "I know why you wanted me to return. You wanted to see my baby die while yours lives! You say I'm out of my mind, but you're the one who's sick!"

She backed away as Princess Revari shouted, "You couldn't stand to see me happy! It just killed you not to be the only one to be loved. I hate you, Vivant! And I'll never forgive you! Never!"

Tearfully, Princess Vivant said, "I don't want to upset you anymore. I'll return to see you when you're feeling better."

"No!" she cried. "You stay away from me and my baby! You're not my sister. Not anymore!"

Princess Vivant, desperate to make amends, reached for her again.

"I'm never going to give up on you, Revari. Once you calm down, you'll see I only want the best for you. I promised you I'd take care of you after Mother died and I always will."

Eyes she'd known and loved for all her life now chilled Princess Vivant.

"Mother is dead! And you...you're dead to me too! Get out! Get out of my face, you treacherous whore!"

She could hear her sister screaming obscenities at her long after she left.

The evening meal was served to Princess Revari by Sergeant Legend.

"Here we are Princess! A hearty bowl of potato chowder, braised beef, potato rolls, and your favorite peach pie."

"Has Oliver eaten?"

Sergeant Legend's smile faltered.

"I wasn't placed in charge of him, Princess, and—"

"Tell me the truth. Is King Dubian..." Her voice broke. "Has he ordered for him to be tortured?"

Her lips pursed, then loudly declared, "To my knowledge, the king has already ordered the Human to be shipped from Platirius. That's all I know."

Before she could respond, the sergeant lightly stepped on her foot. Meeting her eyes, she realized she'd amplified her voice for the cameras. That meant Oliver was still alive.

Further confirming her suspicion, Sergeant Legend whispered, "Pay attention once you reach the bottom of the bowl." She raised her voice again. "The dining staff will clear your supper dishes. I'll return to check on you later." She mouthed something only Princess Revari saw.

She looked at the clock. The night shift would be reporting for duty soon. She didn't have much time to find Oliver and escape.

Adjusting one of her bound wrists to pick up her spoon, she dipped it into the hot, creamy mass of thick broth, flowing with plump chunks of potato and onions. Although it was delicious, she barely noticed.

She wasn't hungry, but she forced herself to eat. She'd need strength to find Oliver and finally rid herself of her deranged family. And this time, she wouldn't be foolish enough to let them find her again.

As she reached the end of the chowder, she saw a blade. Quickly, she tilted the bowl to hide her hands from the camera and caught it in her fingers. She slashed at the bonds as she lowered the spoon into the bowl.

It took three tries before she was freed. She heard a loud blast before darkness descended over the room. It was time.

She stood, yanking the bonds from her wrists, and untied her ankles. Over the years, she'd housed more than a few prisoners. She didn't need light to assist her in finding her way.

Feeling the patterns on the walls, she kept going until she reached the last door of the confinement chamber. Since the power had been temporarily disabled, the soldiers didn't see as she pushed on the door with all her strength. It opened with a soft *click*. He was there! *Oliver*!

"Oliver!" she whispered, running to him.

She gasped, horrified when she saw his unclothed frame. His once beautiful face was severely bruised and slashed open. Deep welts and burns covered his entire body. Gently, she kissed him. His lips felt cold and dry against hers. *Was he...?* She couldn't bear to think it.

"Reve," said Oliver weakly, trying to open his swollen eyes. "Reve, I'm cold. I'm so cold. Let's go home. Please, Reve, I want to go home."

"Shhhh," she said softly, kissing him again. "Don't fret. I'm going to get you out of here. We'll be home soon, okay?"

Raising his hand slowly to feel her lovely face, he grimaced as he tried to smile. Speaking harshly around broken teeth, he said, "I bought the booties you wanted," he whispered. "In soft yellow."

They had argued after he bought a set of orange baby booties.

She thought they were horrific. She told him they reminded her of Halloween and refused to dress their baby in them once it was born. Oliver countered that orange was appropriate since their baby would be born in the fall.

Their arguments were more jesting than genuine disagreements. They never made each other upset. However, the booties were indeed ugly.

"You said you didn't want our baby's feet to look like pumpkins."

His attempt to laugh at their inside joke turned into coughing up copious amounts of blood. With tears streaming down her face, she wiped the blood from his mouth.

Oliver eschewed violence. He wasn't a threat to the Platirians. There was no reason for King Dubian to have inflicted such torment upon him. He did it to hurt her for humiliating him. For being born.

"Don't cry, Reve. This will all be over soon."

On her knees, she gently rocked him back and forth. He felt like a block of ice. She had to get him out of there. Panicking, she looked around for something to dress him in.

A small, brown packet lay in the corner. Easing him down softly, she retrieved it, forcefully tearing it open. It was a Platirian soldier's uniform! She grabbed one arm, frantically placing it into a sleeve. "Oli! Here! I'll help you put this on."

Suddenly, he grabbed her wrist. "Look, Reve," he said softly. His gaze was focused on something above them, past the glass roof of the confinement chamber. Bright stars penetrated the room's darkness. "We're going home."

She looked up, trying to see what captivated him before whirling back to look at him. It was then she saw the light in his eyes fading. *No!*

"Stay with me, Oliver!" she sobbed. "Please, we're going to get out of here, I promise!"

"I love you, Princess Reve. I will...always...love you," he said. As his eyes closed, she felt his body go slack. Moments passed, and she could no longer feel his soul.

'Oliver!" she screamed. "Oliver!"

"Well, what do we have here? A traitorous princess and a dead Human! Today must be my lucky day!"

She looked up into Corporal Fontine's mocking gaze. Sneering, he perused Oliver lying dead in her arms.

"Just imagining you lying with a Human makes me sick to my stomach," he said. "I wasn't good enough for you, but you ran away to be with one of them. Disgusting."

Princess Revari met his gaze. "You're a commoner, Fontine. Your very existence has disgusted me all my life."

He fixed her with a deadly stare. "Still the uppity whore, huh? We'll see how high and mighty you are when your father guts that thing from your belly and tortures it to death!"

"Corporal Fontine!" called a sharp, booming voice.

General Kron stepped into the room. Frightened, Corporal Fontine saluted him. "Yes sir, General Kron! I was just—"

"King Dubian may be at odds with his daughter, but don't think for one minute that elevates you above your place to call her slurs," he barked. "You will be punished for being insolent to a royal!"

"General Kron—" he began.

"Shut up!" he shouted. "You've forgotten your place, soldier! Sergeant Fuller!"

"Yes, General!"

Corporal Fontine withered under the general's intimidating glare. "Lock up Corporal Fontine. I'll deal with him later," he said.

"Yes, sir! Let's go, Fontine!"

Turning his attention from the exiting soldiers, he looked down at her and Oliver.

"I don't blame you for falling in love, but why did it have to be with a Human?"

"I don't owe you any explanations! Why? He's better than you or King Dubian will ever be!"

"Better?" he repeated in disbelief. "A Human? Better than a Platirian? Did you lose your mind along with your honor during your time on Earth, Princess Revari? No Human will ever be better than our race. He may have shown you things your father never has—kindness and compassion—but don't be fooled into thinking Humans are better than your kind."

Hunkering down to peer into her face, he said, "Do you know how we found you?"

"Yes," she said vehemently. "My traitorous sister!"

He bristled at the accusation. "The only traitor to Platirius is you, not my wife. She wants the best for you—to marry a Platirian MaleForm of high status. Not some inferior creature that wasn't fit to clean our boots." He sighed. "I don't know how that will be accomplished now that you bear half of an abomination in your womb!"

Her temper flared. "My baby is no abomination! It's my family—a part of me! And once Oliver and I go home—"

"You *are* home," he countered. "You're where you belong—with your true family. And this *thing*," he said, surveying Oliver in disgust, "is dead. He'll be shipped into the sun along with the rest of the trash we brought here."

Does he mean Oliver's parents and sister? she wondered. *Have they been captured and brought here too?*

Looking into her eyes, he said, "Let me give you a lesson about the true meaning of family. You lowered yourself to live among Humans and thought they loved you. Did you truly believe they'd be loyal to you?"

He shook his head. "Humans do what is in their nature to do. This thing's *family* betrayed you. Yes! One of them told us precisely where you and he were hiding on the condition that we didn't bring him to Platirius with you."

He rose to his full height, staring down at her. "She was foolish enough to believe King Dubian when he promised to leave him alone. She should've known it was a promise he never intended to keep. No Human has ever laid eyes on a Platirian and lived. And now, things are as they should be. Almost. Your father is deciding what to do with the half-thing you'll birth."

"He's not going to touch my baby!" she cried.

"No? Who will stop him? You? Were you able to prevent him from bringing you back to Platirius? Or killing your lover?

You still don't get it, do you? MaleForms know what is best for the WomenForms of Platirius! Your recklessness and unstable emotions created this mess! You never should've run away!"

"I grew tired of being treated like a diseased cur!" she shot back. "Unlike your precious wife who gets anything she wants!"

He twisted his lips in distaste. "Diseased? You were pure before you left Platirius. Now you are infected with the spawn of a Human. You appear to hate her almost as much as your father hates you, but being jealous of her won't solve anything."

Pointing a long finger in her face, he said, "She's not like you. She's loyal to Platirius. She's a lover of peace, not chaos. I'm not saying King Dubian was right for mistreating you, but it's how things are. You've ruined any chance he'll ever accept you."

"He would've never accepted me anyway. Everyone knows this."

"What Platirians know," he said pointedly, "is you betrayed your family. You ran off and spilled our secrets to Humans. That? Is the epitome of treason."

He cocked his head to one side. "To make matters worse, you attempted to escape with him. You would've gladly left your home for a second time to be with him, turning your back on your family. Did you think I didn't know what you'd do next?"

He looked down at the uniform she'd tried to disguise Oliver in. "Whoever helped you get in here will be punished too. You like to believe you're smarter than everyone else, but I am second in command of Platirius for a reason. You, and you alone, brought this on yourself. If you want someone to blame, find a mirror and make sure you're standing front and center!"

"Who's out there?" he bellowed. Four soldiers immediately appeared. Without taking his eyes off her, he said, "Prepare this thing to be shipped out of here. His scent is abhorrent."

She screamed when they ripped Oliver from her arms.

He reached down and pulled her to her feet. "Sergeant Avery!"

"Yes, General Kron!"

"Take Princess Revari back to confinement chamber one and lock her down well."

He turned to her. "I truly hope you will survive this. For my wife's sake, I hope you'll beg for mercy."

Her eyes locked with his. "I'm going to kill you, General Kron," she promised. "And before I do, it is *you* who will beg for mercy!"

His hard stare did little to quell the fury burning inside her.

"The Humans have corrupted your mind. May The One place peace within your soul."

Enraged, she screamed at him when the soldiers grabbed her. Princess Vivant was correct. Her sister had gone completely mad. He vowed to protect her from the mayhem she'd brought down on them.

"Get her out of here," he commanded.

Chapter 4

The time had come for Princess Revari to give birth. King Dubian dispatched Sergeant Legend to watch her until her baby was born.

"As soon as it makes a sound, I must be the first to know. I don't believe I need to remind you what will happen to you if you disregard my orders, WomanForm."

"I understand, King Dubian," said Sergeant Legend.

Sixteen hours later, a tiny InfantForm lay in Princess Revari's arms. It was gray and sickly. Sobbing, she swaddled it, trying to keep it warm. She nearly panicked as it struggled to breathe. King Dubian looked down at the tiny bundle, regretfully shaking his head.

"This is a consequence of disobeying your father," he told her. "The InfantForm is half-Human. It can't survive on our planet. I have no choice but to put it out of its misery."

Nodding to the soldiers, he ordered, "Take it away."

Weakened from giving birth, she tried to hold it tightly to her chest, but failed. Ignoring her pleas for mercy, they took her baby out of the medical chamber.

King Dubian said, "After its shipped out, sedate her and transport her to the Chamber of Despair until she's rehabilitated. She's in no state of mind to be of use to us at this time."

He walked away from the medical chamber, leaving his daughter wailing in anguish.

P rincess Revari spent seven long years in the Chamber of Despair. If it weren't for Sergeant Legend and Gallium sneaking off whenever they could to visit her, she would've entirely descended into madness.

She'd refused to see Princess Vivant who had given birth to three daughters. King Dubian hadn't bothered to visit her. Sergeant Legend was worried she hadn't spoken in years. Suddenly, everything changed.

She began to recover remarkably during the final two years of her stay at the Chamber of Despair. An improved appetite paved the way to building muscle. Soon she was in better shape than many of the Platirian soldiers. Under the guise of learning domestic skills, she trained with one of the best warriors in the Platirian army.

The secret training worked in her favor. King Dubian had made many enemies—on and off Platirius. Aware she planned to get revenge on her father, some were more than eager to assist her in leaving the Chamber of Despair. Her trainer was impressed when she bested him in a duel. In fact, she'd knocked him flat on his back.

"Well done!" he praised. "You are ready!"

"Ready for what?" asked Gallium during one of their secret meetings. "What are you preparing for?"

She was almost finished doing push-ups. "Ninety-eight, ninety-nine, one hundred!"

She jumped up and accepted the cool towel he handed to her. Wiping her face and neck, she said, "General Kron has been fighting on Kikhani for the past three years. He just won the battle and is coming home."

Gallium rolled his eyes. "So, he finally won against them? We'll never hear the end of it."

"Yes, Platirius won, but they barely got out alive. Now that he's escaped death on Kikhani, I intend to introduce him to it after he returns."

Rubbing his hands together, he asked, "You're going to kill General Kron?"

"I am," she said firmly. "He has it coming for what he did to my family."

"I'm all for you ending him. He walks around Platirius as if he owns it, bragging about how he's next in line to be king." He shook his head. "He's disgusting."

"Disgusting...and soon to be stone-cold dead. You'll see. I'm just getting started. And when I'm done, Platirius will never be the same."

He clapped his hands together once. "You'll need help. Sergeant Legend and I would be more than happy to assist you in getting rid of him. And King Dubian too."

Had the king been wiser, he would've learned of her treasonous plans through surveillance. Although she'd been locked away for many years, he still couldn't bear to look at her. Some Platirians speculated it was guilt for not being the father he should've been. Others said it was because she was the spitting image of her mother.

Regardless of the reason, while he slept soundly in his bed late at night, she laid out the plans to send him to an eternal resting place. She and Gallium smiled at each other. The future was beginning to look bright for Princess Revari. For Princess Vivant, however, her nightmare was just beginning.

General Kron's demise was calculated with meticulous precision. By blackmailing Dr. Barrios, she learned he and his family would visit his home planet, Maieman. Since he'd been at war, his parents missed the opportunity to attend the triplets' first Life Celebration. He planned to make it up to them with a surprise trip.

Princess Revari's skill with managing crafts had dramatically improved while isolated from most Platirians. After Gallium helped her sneak out of the Chamber of Despair, she donned a Platirian uniform to move around freely without detection.

She gained access to his personal craft with the assistance of General Legend and rerouted its instructions.

On the day they were set to board, she waited until the family's luggage was loaded on the craft. It was time. She sent a deceptive note to Princess Vivant informing her that the departure time had changed.

This gave her time to get him on the craft alone with an unassuming pilot. His personal pilot had been sedated and locked in a storage closet deep within the Chamber of Despair.

It would be hours before he awakened. Never known to be late, her guest of honor boarded the craft at the expected time and sat down. He spied a round table with a note and a large pitcher filled with his favorite drink. The note made him laugh. Princess Teenah had soiled her tiny gown after filching a small bag of candy from his pocket.

Princess Vivant was strict on cleanliness. She'd bathe her again before they boarded. That gave him a bit of time to relax before the long trip. Putting the note aside, he poured himself a drink. Leaning back in his seat, he sighed with pleasure as he took a healthy gulp of the rich, dark liquid.

It was delicious! He drained the cup and poured more. Before long, he'd drunk the entire pitcher. Twenty minutes later, he wondered what was keeping Princess Vivant. He didn't want to be late getting to Maieman.

I'd better go and find her.

As he started to rise, his legs felt like rubber. The inside of the craft began to swim, causing him to sit back in the seat with a harsh *thud*. He tried to raise his arms. They wouldn't move.

Alarmed, he tried to speak. His tongue felt thick and sluggish in his mouth. When a familiar voice rang out over the low humming of the engine, his heart began to pace rapidly.

"If you've found honey, eat only enough for you, lest you have your fill of it and vomit. Proverbs 25:16," said Princess Revari.

She looked at the empty pitcher and let out a low whistle. "One drink would've done the trick, but you've drunk the entire lot! Tsk. How gluttonous of you!"

She sat down in front of him as his eyes frantically searched around the craft.

"Oh stop that," she admonished. "That silly pilot I paid to sit here until you boarded is long gone. King Dubian has left Platirius on business. Now that was a mistake on your part—trying to leave with his daughter and granddaughters while he was away. I guess he wouldn't have allowed you to take them were he here. He probably thought you wouldn't bring them back, hm? Wow...family drama, I tell you. It's enough to drive you crazy!"

She matched his menacing glare with a smile. "Still tough as ever, are we?"

He watched her smile vanish like the sun during a storm.

"Princess Vivant and your daughters aren't coming. Neither are you going to see your other family on Maieman. Family...what a complicated word. You taught me a lesson about the true meaning of family. Do you remember? I certainly do. That lesson has been burned in my mind for years. It was you who told me about betrayal."

She watched him try to lift his arms. "It's time to pay what you owe, General."

When she stood and sauntered around his seat, his anxiety increased.

"Now, where was I?" she asked, feigning forgetfulness. "Ahh, yes! Family! You helped King Dubian take away my family, so I'm going to take away yours."

Leaning closer, she carefully scanned every angle of his face before looking into his eyes. "Your family will never see this handsome face again. Do you know why? You're going on a little vacation where the weather is always hot and sunny."

Raking a single fingernail down his face unnerved him. For the first time, he flinched.

"I never had the opportunity to raise my baby with my husband. Why should you have the right to raise yours? What makes you better than I?"

He felt her part his knees and the full weight of her knee pressing on his testicles. Enthralled by his muffled screams, she smiled. "I'd rather slit my own throat than watch you become the next king of Platirius."

His eyes flickered as she clapped once.

"Well, now I don't have to, do I? No, I sure don't because you're going to fry like bacon!"

His attempts to speak only succeeded in making incoherent sounds. She rose from the seat, fascinated by the frantic look in his eyes and cocked a hand to her ear.

"What's that? Do I hear you begging for mercy, General? Oh, don't tell me you're protesting going on vacation. After all the hard work you've done for Platirius, I'd say you had this coming! You thought the sun would be good enough for my husband. Now you'll get to see it too."

Looking down at him triumphantly, she said, "Finally, you'll know how I felt all those years ago. Helpless. Angry. Desperate. I wish I could see the look on your face right before you start sizzling, knowing you'll never see your family again."

She leaned in close to his face and placed her hands on his broad shoulders.

"I'll leave you with words of comfort. I will kill Princess Vivant too—oh be quiet and listen! You're so rude! I'm going to kill her right in front of your babies. Then? I'll draft them into my army. Does that work for you, brother-in-law?"

Holding his eyes, she said, "I gave your wife a final note from you. She thinks you've been called away at the last minute for a battle. I ended it with, 'Goodbye, my love!' It's generic and boring, but it works in a pinch. Adios, General Kron. You've just won an all-expenses paid trip to Hell!"

No, he thought. *It can't end this way! Vivant and our ChildForms need me! If I don't stop her, she'd kill them all!*

His body refused to respond to his desperate attempts to free himself.

After barely escaping Kikhani alive, I've returned home to die at the hands of an insane WomanForm!

She turned to the motherboard and started the engine, leaving him unable to stop the fate awaiting him. Renewed hope soared within her watching the craft soar across Space. There was still so much left to do...and so little time to do it.

Chapter 5

General Lyric cradled the empty bottle that once held the CallePepper. In her heart, she knew it was the reason for Queen Vivant's sudden descent into a mental spiral. It needed to be analyzed.

Did she trust Simonius to do it? No. She suspected he had more than a few secrets waiting to be exposed. She didn't have time to concentrate on him. Her first order of business was to restore her back to health.

She entered Platineous's elaborate research chamber and found Sonee seated at a massive desk.

"What are you working on?" she asked.

Sonee looked up at her, noting the bags under her eyes. Since Queen Vivant had become ill, none of the Vivacians had been getting much sleep.

"I managed to take a bit of the Human's skin before they locked him away in the confinement chamber."

She removed a pile of books from a chair and motioned for her to sit down. Grateful for her compassion, General Lyric sank into the soft chair.

"There's a strange substance in his blood. It's not anything found on Earth. It looks as if it comes from our planet, but I can't figure out how or where he found it."

"Maybe he didn't find it," said General Lyric. "Maybe it found him."

Sonee turned to look at her. "What do you mean by that?"

She produced a small tin. "Look at this. It's CallePepper. Approximately three months ago, Gallium started bringing tons of it to Platineous."

Sonee placed her chin in her hands. "But didn't Queen Revari throw a tantrum and say Platineous wasn't allowed to eat her precious food?"

"Exactly! I wasn't suspicious of this until I noticed her sprinkling a lot of it on Queen Vivant's food at the DeathCeremony and even afterward. Every time she ate, Queen Revari was adamant about adding this to her food. She put on a show about her needing to keep up her strength. Why? She's never cared about her staying healthy before."

"Maybe she wasn't trying to make her healthy," said Sonee. "Maybe she was drugging her."

They shared a look. General Lyric had begun to doubt she could prove Queen Revari was behind her sister's malady. Sonee was the brightest researcher in both realms. If anyone could team up with her to help the queen, it was her.

"Gallium's title is royal chief gardener, but he's much more than that," said Sonee.

She pulled up his profile on the screen.

"He's actually a chemist and a genius one at that. He can take any plant and make it into various things. Food, drugs—nothing is off limits to him. And he's been doing it for many years for Queen Revari. Who's to say he didn't create it specifically to drug her?"

"Except we've all eaten it," said General Lyric. "It hasn't affected us the way it affected her."

Sonee continued reading his profile. "Drug response levels differ depending on the body it interacts with. Maybe the CallePepper produced changes in her system that wouldn't work the same in our bodies. It's certainly possible. We're both aware Queen Revari doesn't give one hoot about what happens to her."

Sonee tapped his face with a pen. "She's wanted her out of the way for a long time. He also uses some of the plants he grows and turns them into substances to be used as weapons for war. Our technology is far more advanced than other realms. Everyone on Rubarius is loyal to her. With no one to look over his shoulder, he could've easily designed it to hurt only Queen Vivant. Does that make sense?"

General Lyric nodded. "It does. We have to stop her from taking it. Could we create something of our own as a substitute?"

"Sure, but we can't have her stop taking it cold turkey. The consequences could be fatal. We'd have to wean her off slowly."

Sonee sat thinking for a moment, drumming her tiny fingers on the desk. "I've observed her at mealtimes. She won't eat anything without it. If she's truly hooked on it, she may struggle with addiction for the rest of her lifespan."

Punching numbers into the system, Sonee said, "I'll run some tests on it to try and figure out exactly how it was designed. Once I expose what we're working with, I may be able to synthesize an anecdote to counteract its effects."

She thought it would take days for Sonee to find a solution. It took hours.

"I've got it!" cried Sonee. "I think I know what Gallium did to the CallePepper!"

She squeezed her shoulder. "Sonee, that colossal brain of yours never ceases to amaze me."

"I was right," said Sonee. "Unadulterated CallePepper is a vegetable, nothing more. Plants contain water, cellulose, fats, starches, and proteins. But when you add different substances, a newly created mutation can alter internal stimuli. I suspect this is why she's been experiencing excessive hunger, thirst, and those erratic mood swings."

She got up and removed a couple of books from a high shelf. "While I'm not one hundred percent certain how he mutated it, I've created an antidote. If we mix eighty percent of the substance I've designed with twenty percent of the CallePepper, her body might respond more favorably to it. Then, we'll continue decreasing the dosage over time."

She carefully scanned one of the books until she found what she wanted. "As her body goes through a withdrawal phase, there's less risk of her body going into shock, having a heart attack, or even worse, dying. We need to switch his version with the formula I've made. After he brings a new box, we'll intercept it from the dining chamber and replace it with the antidote."

"Then her powers may return," said General Lyric. "I think the CallePepper somehow muted them. She should've been able to read Aja's mind and discover she'd been copulating with Simonius long before the DeathCeremony, but she didn't. That means they've been giving it to her right under our noses. We didn't find out something was wrong until her behavior changed."

"Exactly. The withdrawal period may be tough for her to experience and even tougher for us to watch. No Revaltians should be allowed around her. If they see she's getting better, they'll report it to General Legend, who'll report it to Queen Revari. We have to make her think she's still too sick to interfere in her takeover of Earth. She needs sufficient time to recover."

"That won't be a problem. General Legend is aware that I know what she's been doing with Simonius. She won't come anywhere near Platineous. Most of the Revaltians are on Earth with Queen Revari, and the few remaining here are too busy to check on us."

Sonee clapped her hands together. "They're collecting souls. You can see the souls ascend and descend at all times of the day and night over Rubarius. The entire realm is illuminated when they dive deep into the soil. Rubarius is getting stronger!"

She slid on a pair of gloves and handed some to General Lyric. "We don't have much time. We have to get her better so she can stop Queen Revari."

They gently placed the antidote in vials.

"They messed with the wrong queen," said Sonee. "It's time we give Queen Revari's lapdogs a taste of their own medicine!"

When the new batch of CallePepper arrived, they switched it with her antidote and swore the dining staff to secrecy. Two weeks went by with no change in the queen's condition. Sonee began to wonder if her theory was correct.

Two more days passed. General Lyric and the Vivacians stayed by her side, trying to be optimistic about the future of Platineous. An hour after she had retired for the night, a bloodcurdling scream sounded through the east wing of the palace. It was Queen Vivant.

Sergeant Thea ran from her bed chamber. "She's having a nightmare! I can't wake her up!"

General Lyric ran to her and found her thrashing amongst the bed linens, heavily perspiring. Crying out against an unseen enemy, she settled a bit when her forehead was bathed with a cool cloth.

"Queen Vivant, can you hear me?" asked General Lyric.

I n the recesses of her mind, her home and the army she loved were as distant as the space between Heaven and Hell. She opened her eyes and saw tall, lush green grass. A voice to called her. Turning slightly, she couldn't determine its direction.

She stopped to pick a beautiful red rose and inhaled its sweet fragrance. Its petals fell away until the bare thorns were left. The thorny stem took a life of its own, encircling her wrist and pricking her skin, causing blood to flow freely down her arm.

"Vivant!" said the voice. "Vivant, I'm over here!"

She followed the voice until she came face to face with...

Her face brightened. "Lucian! My love! You're here!"

Running as fast as she could, she raised her arms to embrace him. An unseen force stopped her shortly before she reached him. Two former lovers, separated by death, faced each other. He wasn't the Lucian she knew. His eyes were dark and empty. Troubled.

Her eyes searched his face. "I thought I'd never see you again. Is this...the afterlife? Am I staying here with you?"

He shook his head solemnly. "No. Your time has not yet come."

She wanted to touch him so badly. "Have you seen our daughters, Lucian? Are they here?"

His eyes were devoid of the warmth she remembered. "No, Vivant. I've been alone here. No time or space exists in this realm."

Horrified, she reached out to touch him again and found she couldn't. She wanted nothing more than to hold him in her arms. For the first time, she felt lonely in his presence. She didn't like this place—it was dark and cold. She knew that he, too, had been lonely. Her heart ached for him.

"We were wrong, Vivi. What we did to Revari was inexcusable. We should've stood up to King Dubian and told him we weren't going to help him. She had a right to live her life the way she wanted."

"No," she said, slowly backing away. "You agreed with me about bringing her home. She was a princess of Platirius living among Humans. It was disgraceful!"

He moved toward her. "Was it? When was she ever treated as your equal? What was the real reason for wanting her to return to Platirius?"

"I wanted her to have the best! Lucian, you know this! We are Platirians! We've never lowered ourselves to live among inferior races! She wasn't herself. Although she couldn't see it, she needed me. I helped her see reason!"

He shook his head. "No. You helped her to be locked away for several long years. And you helped your father become so drunk with insanity that he murdered her baby. How did it help her to lose her child in such a callous way?"

She sucked in her breath, her stomach turning into knots. "Why have you turned on me? You've never spoken to me this way before. You're my husband, not hers. Why are you taking her side over mine? How could you be so disloyal?"

"You're the last one who should speak of disloyalty."

Her temper finally got the best of her.

"I have been loyal to the throne of Platirius for my entire life! I have never neglected my duty! How dare you accuse me of betraying my planet!"

She felt as if she were talking to stone. She hadn't expected ever to see him again, but he wasn't the MaleForm she'd fallen in love with.

"I haven't accused you of betraying Platirius. I'm asking how you stood by and watched your sister's life fall apart with no remorse? Before she ran away, did you do anything to protect her from your father's wrath?"

He'd never spoken to her so acrimoniously in all the years of their marriage.

"I tried to persuade Father to treat her with kindness! He wouldn't listen to me!"

He snorted. "If you knew he was adamant about destroying her life, why didn't you let her be happy away from him?"

She was silent.

"Answer the question, Vivant. Why did you want her to return to Platirius after you discovered she'd found happiness?!"

Trembling, she looked around for a way to escape but found none.

"Answer me."

Why is he attacking me? "Don't speak to me like I'm one of your soldiers! I'm your wife and your equal! I don't take orders from you!"

His unrelenting gaze was fixated on her. Instinctively, she winced. "There's nowhere to run and hide here. You will answer for what you've done!"

Maybe if I tell him what he wants to hear, he'll leave me alone. "Because I couldn't abide Father's suffocating ways, alright?"

Exasperated by his questions, she said, "Without Revari around, he turned his attention on me! I had to be perfect in the way I spoke and dressed. And...he'd changed his mind about allowing me to marry you! He said it would be better if I remained unmarried to care for him as he aged. I wasn't born to be his NurseForm! I wanted a life of my own!"

The empty look in his eyes made her shudder. "There it is. You sacrificed your sister's happiness for your own. When she returned to Platirius, he invented ways to make her miserable. You stood by while her husband and child were murdered, knowing it was wrong. How have you managed to live with yourself?"

Tears spilled from her eyes. "That's not fair," she whispered.

"Oh, it's fair. You had a choice. You could have come to Maieman with me to live. We would've been happier without your father controlling our every move. But you didn't want that."

"You wouldn't have been king had we left!"

His steel gray eyes ripped open her soul.

"And nothing was more important than that. Not our happiness. Not our ChildForms' happiness. You wanted to be

85

the queen of Platirius—no matter the cost! And now you've paid for it with our daughters' lives."

She held up her hands, silently pleading with him. "You're being cruel! You can't blame me for our daughters' deaths. I gave them everything I had to give!"

"Jewelry, clothing, crafts—silly materialistic things they couldn't take with them when they died."

He waved his hand dismissively. "You were so focused on throwing them a silly Life Celebration that you failed to keep them safe! For all your contempt for Humans, couldn't you see the danger of having one roaming around Platineous? Why didn't you send him away once you discovered him?"

"We were conducting an investigation—"

"An investigation for what?"

"To—to find out how he came to Platirius!"

"He didn't need to stay for you to do that. How many times did I drill the protocol into your head? Any outsiders were to be immediately removed from our lands *before* an investigation was conducted to reduce the risk of contamination."

He pointed an accusatory finger at her. "You broke protocol by allowing the Human to stay. And for what? So you could find a way to tie him to Revari and dethrone her. You wanted Platirius to reunite so you could have it for yourself. Once again, you didn't think she was fit to be your equal!"

Unable to bear any more of his scrutiny, she looked off into the distance.

"That's not true!" she whispered.

"Isn't it? Look around you."

He opened his arms wide. "Here you stand out in the open with nothing except truth staring you in the face! When are you going to admit you were jealous of her? That's why you wouldn't allow her to exist away from Platirius. It's why you didn't lose an ounce of sleep when she lost her family, and it's why you felt she deserved to be locked away for being crazy when you knew full well she wasn't!"

She shook her head. "No, I love Revari. Even if Father didn't, I loved her! She's my sister. How could I not?"

"You loved her as long as she was the despised child of your father. As a helpless ChildForm, she depended on you for love and guidance. But as she got older, she grew stronger and braver. She challenged your father by refusing to allow him to control her life."

She defiantly looked into his soulless eyes. "I've always been proud of my sister—-"

He cut her off. "She earned her place in the Platirian army, collecting heads while you allowed him to control everything down to forcing us to have separate bedrooms! She did something you never could—she stood up to him. You were jealous of that. Once we married, she resigned from the army because she didn't want to report to me or you. That enraged you."

She tried to walk away but her feet refused to move.

"You wanted her—no, needed her—to be under your authority to feel superior to her. After King Dubian died, you were forced to rule Platirius with her. Word was dispatched about his illness. You could've left the training anytime you wanted. But you didn't. You secretly hoped he would die so you would be appointed queen."

"I refuse to listen to any more of this nonsense! You were the one who loved to hop from battle to battle, leaving me alone with our ChildForms! How dare you stand there and accuse me of—"

"Then you returned and found nothing was as you expected," he continued. "When Fate destined you to rule only half of it, that wasn't good enough for you—you wanted it all! Finding a connection between her and the Human was your way to get exactly what you wanted. But it didn't work out as you planned. How does it feel to know you failed as a queen and as a mother?"

Her spirit shattered like glass. Her tears fell on the harsh terrain. She didn't want to believe any of the things he said but...it was true. She had always run from the truth. Now it had come to claim its place.

For the first time since seeing him in her dreams, his visage softened. "True healing begins with taking responsibility for your actions. No wrong will ever be righted without accountability. Admit you've always wanted Platirius for yourself."

Moving toward her didn't close the distance between them. He couldn't meet her in her world, nor could she journey into his. Death was permanent. Desolate. She had never felt so alone.

"It's something you've loved more than me. More than our daughters. And more than your father and sister. It was the power that sated you more than love."

She hung her head in defeat. "It's true. I wanted to be the sole queen of Platirius."

"And still you are not. You sacrificed everyone you loved for power."

She shook her head furiously. "Not my daughters. I knew I could prove the Revaltians were behind the Human's arrival on Platirius. I never expected they'd die! If I had known, if I could turn back time, I would! I'd never sacrifice my babies for the throne."

"You didn't mind sacrificing Revari's baby."

"No, I didn't," she snapped. "Is that what you want to hear?"

"The truth must be confronted if you're going to lead Platineous with honor and dignity. Authentic leadership begins with honesty and ends with responsibility. I have not come to shame you. You must take accountability for what you've done. It's the only way you'll heal."

He waved his hand, displaying Platirius as it was before it split. She surveyed the breathtaking gardens nestled around the grand compound she and Queen Revari grew up in. Happy Platirians bustled through various chambers, greeting each other as they faced a new day.

Families lived together instead of on opposite sides of the planet. It was a united Platirius—something she'd prayed would exist again.

"I wish for everyone to be healed," he said. "After millions of years of cruelty and madness permeating Platirius, it deserves a leader of pure heart and selfless ambition. Now that you've faced your fears, you are almost ready. I must leave you now."

"No. Don't go. Please stay with me," she begged.

Shaking his head, he backed slowly away from her. "I cannot. My journey is no longer among the living."

Her tears flowed like a river. Would she never touch him again?

"I miss you."

"I've missed you too. We'll be together again in the realm of The One, but not now. The time has come for you to learn...and grow. You have far too many who trust in you. Depend on you. You can't afford to fail them."

With a heavy heart, she watched him fade away. Struggling to forgive her imperfections while begging for forgiveness from The One, she vowed to free herself of the burdens she had carried.

She wanted to be a better sister and an honorable leader for her realm. But she didn't know how.

Darker days passed for Queen Vivant. Her body continued purging the toxins of the CallePepper, causing a level of physical pain that she hadn't experienced before.

She writhed, screamed, and called out to shadows that weren't there. Helpless, her loyal subjects watched, unable to assist her when her body yearned for more unadulterated CallePepper.

She screamed again before welcoming the refuge of unconsciousness. Unlike the ill-lit, inhospitable place where she'd met General Kron, she awakened in a splendid world filled with light and breathtaking acres of jeweled land.

"Vivant!"

Where have I heard that voice? It was familiar...and a balm for her soul.

"Come to me, Vivant!"

This time, she was in a breathtaking orchard of lemons. Leaning her head back, she welcomed the warm scent of sunshine and the energizing, tangy scent of lemons.

She walked among the trees, enchanted by the beauty of everything around her. Someone sat on a brilliant blue cushion, her legs crossed as she gazed lovingly at her.

"Mother?! Mother, it's you!" she said, running at full speed toward her.

Queen Dellah stood, encasing her daughter in a warm hug.

Queen Vivant cried tears of joy. "I can't believe it! You're here!"

"Yes, I am," said Queen Dellah. "I came because you needed me."

Pushing her back to gaze at her, she realized she'd forgotten how beautiful her mother was.

Queen Dellah took in every detail of her face. "It's not easy being queen, is it?"

"Oh Mother, I've made so many mistakes," she said miserably.

"Living with your father hasn't been easy for you. I'm sorry I wasn't around to shield you from his ways."

Unable to meet her eyes, she lowered her head. "It's not your fault, Mother."

The former matriarch of Platirius placed her hands on the young queen's shoulders. "Nor is it Revari's fault, Vivant."

Queen Vivant averted her eyes. After being ripped open and exposed by her husband, she wasn't ready for another re-hashing with her mother.

"Dubian blamed her for my demise all her life. He unleashed his hurt and rage on my baby, never realizing life doesn't give us a choice in whether we stay or go. When we are called Home, we must answer it. There is no negotiating with The One."

Cupping her chin, she lifted it until her eyes met hers. "And you, daughter, you also blamed your sister for losing me. It wasn't fair to her or you. After I gave birth to you, the royal physicians told me I'd never carry again. They were wrong."

She closed her eyes when her hands closed over hers. It felt wonderful to feel her mother's touch again.

"Discovering I was carrying your sister was one of the best moments of my life. No one thought I would die, not even me. How many times have I wanted to hold both of you close to me when you hurt? Crossing the barrier between the worlds of the living and the dead cannot happen without His permission."

Queen Vivant squeezed her hands. "Mother...have you been with us all this time?"

"Oh yes. That's what MotherForms do—watch over their babies. I've had to watch with no power to intervene...until now. Vivant, you are a queen. You have been honored with a position not just of birthright but out of duty to The One."

"Come," said Queen Vivant. "Let us go. I didn't have enough time to walk in our gardens with you."

She experienced a peace she hadn't felt in years as they strolled around the vast landscape.

"When you're a queen, there is no room for pettiness and unforgiveness," said Queen Dellah. "You'll be bestowed with an even greater responsibility. You must be ready to claim the place you are destined for."

"How can The One still want me to be Protector? I'm not perfect, Mother. I haven't performed my duties as gallantly as you. I'm so...ashamed of myself. I'm ashamed of the pain I've caused Revari. My daughters. My husband. My army. My Platirians. I've lived as an arrogant shell of a royal—drinking ambition like the finest wine. I've made everyone so miserable."

Queen Dellah took her face in her hands. "You recognize the wrongs you've done. Some never do. They go about life hurting and continuing to hurt everyone they encounter. Your sister is one of them. She's learned to fashion her pain into a brush, painting chaos and disorder on every one of life's canvases. It is up to you to teach her how to let go of the past and embrace the future that awaits her."

An image of Queen Revari and the family she'd helped to ruin flashed across Queen Vivant's mind. "She lost everything because of me. I was selfish and jealous that she loved a Human more than I. If I could change the past, I would, but it's too late. How could I ask her to forgive me? More importantly, how do I learn to forgive myself?"

Queen Dellah moved a lock of hair from her face. "Forgiveness comes from The One and from within. It will be difficult, but you must continue trying to reach your sister. When she falls back, you move forward. Keep telling her you love her. Let her see how remorseful you are for what happened. You're not ChildForms anymore. You've become the two most powerful WomenForms in Platirius's history."

When Queen Vivant's head bowed again, she lifted it, wiping her tears away.

"You've surpassed the most significant achievements of all the kings of Platirius. There's so much more for you both to do, and you cannot do it alone. For the sake of Platirius, you must come together. Platirius has always been one. It was never meant to be separated. Neither were you and Revari. Pain has brought you to me, but the path to freedom is redemption."

They rested their heads together.

"Humble yourself before The One. Confess to Him with your heart and allow Him to guide you. I wish I could tell you the worst is behind you, but I cannot. You and your sister will need each other, for Platirius will need both of you to survive."

A sheen of tears misted in her eyes. She wished they could stay together forever.

"I understand, Mother. I will make you proud of me, I promise."

Queen Dellah's eyes shone vibrantly. "I'm already proud of you, Vivant. I have been since the day you were born. And I always will be. Go now...and claim your destiny."

They held each other tightly, neither wanting to let go. Queen Vivant opened her eyes and found herself alone. It was time to let go of the past.

Unaware Queen Vivant was recovering, Revari connected with all the Revaltians she'd brought to Earth on a conference call.

"How many more souls are needed before we can begin the absorption process?" she asked.

"Less than two hundred," said Jia.

Revari eased back in her chair, sighing with satisfaction. Finally, it was going to be over. She'd accomplished what all the past rulers of Platirius had failed to do—conquer Earth. She hoped King Dubian was spinning in Hell over her victory.

"Then let's finish this. I'm eager to return to Platirius and see it as one again."

I t took less than half a day for the final soul to be swapped in exchange for a faulty promise of Allebri. Platirians watched Rubarius take on an illuminating sheen. The ground shook violently, sending them running for cover. The trembling was reminiscent of when King Dubian died.

Gallium ran out of the gardening chamber and looked toward Space.

Is it possible that Rubarius and Platineous will finally be no more?

Before his eyes, both realms began to move together with lightning speed. A whirlwind of colors swept through them, mixing new hues and making things anew.

A loud explosion sounded from deep within the grounds. General Lyric reached Queen Vivant just before the palace exploded. The queen was thrust into the atmosphere before the horrified gazes of frightened Platirians.

"It's Queen Vivant!" said Dora Reese running out of the crumbling dining chamber. "She's flying over Platirius!"

She flew upward, soaring higher into Space. As every Platirian watched, she became engulfed in a blaze of blue lightning as Platirius became...*one.*

Earth, veiled in the same strange blue bolts, careened toward Platirius.

She's done it! thought General Legend. *Queen Revari has reunited Platirius! She's won!*

Her smile faded when Queen Vivant's eyes opened, blazing a fiery blue. "What's she doing?!"

Queen Vivant flew toward Earth with outstretched hands. Thunderstruck Platirians witnessed her stop Earth from moving in mid Space! She hovered between Earth and her planet, pushing Earth away from Platirius with all her might. The brilliant blue flames grew more intense as she continued pushing.

The Surveyors' voice drifted across Space. *"Earth cannot fall..."*

"Queen Vivant," screamed General Lyric. "You have to let go! You'll be killed!"

But she didn't release Earth. She couldn't. Instead, she she held on with all of her strength, shouting when the flames continued their roaring fury through her and Earth. Suddenly, the walls of Space opened, and a Hand reached down and bolstered her up. Then both were surrounded by dazzling platinum flames.

The Platirians stood solemnly, believing they were watching the death of Queen Vivant. But the realm of The One energized her, and Earth slowly pivoted back to its original place.

Four horsemen descended from Heaven, rushing toward the four billion souls remaining on Earth. As foretold by the book of Revelation, the Humans braced themselves for the coming of the Apocalypse.

The Hand released her and began to write among the stars, high above Platirius. She flew down to the crowd. Together, they watched the Hand determine the future of Platirius. She read aloud what had been decreed by The One.

Platirius is as it was...one planet. One race. The near fall of Earth gave rise to the redemption of Platirius as the most powerful authority in the galaxy, second only to the realm of The One. As it was initiated into practice by the forces of evil, the rise of Queen Revari Ava Amorous has ended. Let all who are present hear the will of The One...

The former Queen of Rubarius ended numerous lives to increase her power, while the former Queen of Platineous sought to give the ultimate sacrifice—her own life—to save Earth. Let the halls of Heaven and Platirius echo this sacred decree: On this day, General Revari, daughter of King Dubian and Queen Dellah, will not ascend to the throne of Platirius.

She is hereby rendered as its servant under the indomitable reign of its rightful ruler, the Protector of Earth and Platirius, Queen Vivant. What The One Has Willed, No Being Shall Abrogate.

All watched the Hand return into the wall of Space as the writing materialized in Platirius's Eternal Hall of Records. Platirians, who the gulf between Rubarius and Platineous had long separated, embraced each other with joy and laughter.

All except the ones who remained loyal to General Revari: Major Legend, Gallium, and Dr. Barrios were nowhere to be found while Simonius hatched a plan to save his neck.

W hile the rest of the Platirians were distracted, he crept into the confinement chamber, seeking Aja.

Aja had witnessed the proclamation of The One. Now that Queen Vivant had been appointed as Platirius's sole ruler, she feared for her life.

"Aja!"

Tears of relief sprang to her eyes. "Simonius! What are you doing here?"

"I've come to break you out of here. We have to leave before Queen Vivant kills us!"

When he reached for her, she grabbed his hand and held it to her face. "I thought you'd forgotten about me," she sobbed.

"How could I? You're the love of my life!" His eyes searched her face. "Have they treated you well? Have you eaten?"

She shook her head. "Not yet."

He searched his uniform. "Here," he said, handing her a small flask. "It's not much, but I took it from the dining chamber. It's peach nectar."

Grateful for the small boon, she took it, smiling at him. "This is so kind of you. Thank you."

"It's my pleasure! Now we have to find a way out of here!"

She quickly drank the nectar. It was sweet, cool, and delicious. After she drained the flask, a burning sensation filled her throat. Unable to breathe, she clawed at her neck. Thick, frothy, purple foam bubbled from her mouth. *Ashion!* Stricken, she looked at him in disbelief.

"You didn't think I'd destroy my life for an idiotic WomanForm like you, did you? You're all the same. Tell you a few lies, and you'll be willing to give up everything you hold dear. Just like my MotherForm." Pressing his face against the glass door, he said, "It was worth the wait seeing you like this."

For the first time, she saw his true nature. The ugliness he'd carefully concealed in his heart showed plainly on his handsome face. She lay dying, finally realizing General Lyric had been right. How could she have jeopardized everything for someone so evil?

He waited until he saw no signs of life in her body before calmly removing the flask and wiping away traces of his prints on the door. He'd silenced Aja for eternity. Now he had one more mouth to close—Major Legend.

M ajor Legend was less trusting than Aja. She refused to eat or drink anything he offered. He flew into a rage when she ignored the flask in his outstretched hand.

"You have just as much to lose as I do!" he snarled. "We have to run away! You and Queen Revari were demoted to General and Major! Do you not understand Queen Vivant will kill us both?"

She smirked. *MaleForms are truly the dumber SexForm,* she thought.

"No, she'll kill you. I've been loyal to Queen—General Revari longer than you've been alive. You may be worthless to her, but I'll never be!"

"Oh? How much worth will you have once she finds out you helped murder her son?"

She stared at him. "You! You sneaky MaleForm! You tried to probe my mind!"

He laughed. "Not tried. Did! And I saw you take the baby away from her. Then you stood by as it was murdered. You're in no position to turn your back on me now!"

She crossed her arms over her breasts. "You don't know half of what you think you know. You only saw a small part of my mind but I assure you, my past deeds will save my life. I can't say the same for you!"

Laughing in his face, she said, "You'd better run with your tail between your legs and try to get off Platirius before General Revari returns. Or before Queen Vivant finds you! You won't receive any help from me."

Fury clouded his handsome face.

"You'll regret betraying me, Legend. Wait and see!"

Chapter 6

He found Dr. Barrios in the research chamber. He was less helpful than Major Legend.

"You fool! Do you realize what you've done?"

Simonius sat down and stretched his legs across one of the large tables. "I know precisely what I'm doing, Dr. Barrios."

"I doubt it! You've placed every MaleForm here in danger!"

Simonius laughed. "Every? There are only three of us. We've been under the thumb of WomenForms for too many years. We have zero power to take a piss when we want!"

Dr. Barrios continued as if he hadn't heard him.

"And for what? For the chance to spread Major Legend's thighs? What? Putting the pipe to that Vivacian soldier and the Revaltians, two at a time, wasn't good enough? You know full well that copulation is against the rules. It's the one rule that'll get MaleForms killed. I thought you were smarter than that!"

Simonius fixed him with a penetrating gaze. "Oh I *am*. I'm more intelligent than you'll ever know. Do you really think I'd throw away my life for a chance to lie with them? For all your years of advanced education, you're not the sharpest pin in the craft."

"I'm not the one copulating with WomenForms," said Dr. Barrios through gritted teeth. "I don't think you have room to talk about intellect."

Simonius shrugged. "My motivation was lust, nothing more. They're beautiful WomenForms, but none are worth more than the time it takes to spill our fluids inside them." He stared at Dr. Barrios, wondering if he should tell him what he'd discovered when he probed Major Legend's mind.

Copulation was forbidden on Platirius for a good reason. Platirius was built on misogynistic leadership and dark magic. For some Platirian MaleForms, copulation awakened deep-seated hatred of WomenForms. Ingrained social norms inspired them to value power and privilege over emotional connection.

General Kron and even King Dubian had loved and cherished their wives, but treated the rest of the WomenForms horribly. For them, the Mass Deaths ended millions of years of tyranny and discrimination.

To Simonius, the unjust act destroyed countless innocent lives. He still mourned the MaleForms sent to destruction with King Dubian. His father, his brothers, and friends. Some of them hadn't lived a full three months.

General Revari and Queen Vivant had viciously murdered them all. He hadn't forgotten or forgiven King Dubian's daughters. For many years, he'd toed the line. Keeping his eyes cast downward, he performed whatever tasks he was ordered to complete.

When the sensual urges began to overtake him, he'd lost the battle to fight them off and found a few of the WomenForms had been more than willing to lie with him.

General Revari was a master of war—and revenge. If she discovered he'd been copulating with WomenForms in both armies, she'd throw him in the Flames of Justice herself. Although she'd rather slit your throat than admit it, her reign had been reminiscent of her father's.

He longed for the days when Platirius thrived under the leadership of MaleForms. He couldn't face another day wondering when Queen Vivant—or even worse, General Revari—would kill him. Now he had an ace up his sleeve.

Spinning his favorite pin in his fingers, he said, "Did you know General Revari bore a son?"

The doctor gaped at him. *How does he know?*

"I'm aware, Simonius. Who do you think was called to deliver it?"

"So you know what happened to him?"

What is he getting at? "Her son has long been dead and burned."

It wasn't a discussion he wished to have with him. To even speak of it was treasonous.

A gleam of triumph shone in Simonius's eyes. "No, Dr. Barrios. Her son didn't die."

A wave of nausea rose in Dr. Barrios. "You are asking to be executed. We never speak of such secrets! King Dubian killed the InfantForm. I was there—he sent him into the sun."

Simonius smiled. "He murdered an InfantForm. Not the son of General Revari."

Dr. Barrios rubbed his eyes. "What in Platirius are you talking about?"

"Well," said Simonius, leaning back in his chair and intertwining his fingers, "when we sleep with WomenForms, we can see their memories. It's been so long for you. Perhaps you've forgotten."

Dr. Barrios bristled. He was in no mood for Simonius's gaslighting. "I remember, Simonius. I was copulating with WomenForms before you were born."

Simonius scowled. He was almost as arrogant as General Revari and loved being the center of attention. "Are you going to listen or not?"

He stared Dr. Barrios down for a moment. "Thank you. Now as I was saying, when copulating with Major Legend, I saw her switch a sick baby MaleForm with General Revari's healthy InfantForm. Then she transported him to Earth."

He paused dramatically, savoring the knowledge he'd learned about General Revari's past.

"She gave him to a Human woman whose baby had already died. And for many years, she secretly visited Earth, keeping a close eye on him. She never lost track of him. She believes I don't know the truth because I lied to her, accusing her of murdering him so she'd help me escape."

He crossed his ankles. "But I saw everything when I probed her mind. King Dubian forbade you from giving the general a remedy so she wouldn't suffer. After she passed out from the pain, it gave Major Legend the perfect opportunity to swap them."

Smiling slyly at the doctor, he said, "I've often wondered how you survived the Mass Deaths. What do you think she'll do once she finds out you played a role in her son's demise?

His thinly veiled threat hit the mark. Although Dr. Barrios's face remained impassive, Simonius sensed he had the upper hand.

"Well, anyway, when she woke up, the sick one was lying next to her. After the king arrived, he seized it and had the general dragged in front of everyone to witness what she thought was her son being sent to his death."

Dr. Barrios's hand wrapped around a blade. If what Simonius said was true, he had to be stopped. If General Revari discovered he'd assisted King Dubian—

"Only Major Legend knew the InfantForm he murdered didn't belong to her. She never told her and purposely kept memories of him hidden due to Queen Vivant's ability to read all our minds. She couldn't risk being exposed but he lives. He's half-Human, half-Platirian."

"It...can't be!" said Dr. Barrios.

Simonius, deep in thought, didn't see him advancing towards him.

"Oh, it's true. I've seen him. He's a brain specialist."

Dr. Barrios's grip tightened around the blade. "Even if this is true, what does it have to do with you?"

Simonius's tone was confident. "I plan to bring him here."

"What?!"

"The One declared General Revari couldn't be the ruler of Platirius, but He never said her son couldn't. If he challenges Queen Vivant for the throne, he may win! Think about it... Platirius is whole again. If he took his rightful place, our planet would be under a MaleForm ruler again—as it should be!"

He stared at Simonius, wondering how he'd managed to keep his ambitious nature a secret. "You...are crazy! Neither Queen Vivant or General Revari would ever allow a MaleForm—even her own son—to rule Platirius! Now that Queen Vivant has been appointed, Platirius is hers! How do you think you're going to bring him here?"

He realized he'd worked side by side with Simonius for years and still had no idea who he really was.

"Second, this kid is half-Human. He's not a full Platirian. Which means he doesn't have the full power his ancestors had. Queen Vivant would mop the floor with him if he challenged her for Platirius."

He'd always hated his smugness. Although he and Gallum shared an amicable relationship, Simonius irritated him.

"And? Ashion for brains, he can't take the throne unless both sisters are dead. Queen Vivant has the authority to control the Vivacians and all the Revaltians who aren't in fear of dying for copulating with you! You have no one on your side."

"Not yet," said Simonius sanguinely.

"Not ever. If you think Gallium and I will go along with your hare-brained scheme, you best think again! I'm not going to die following behind a fool too stupid to realize what he has!"

"And what do we have, Dr. Barrios? Bowing and scraping at the hands of WomenForms?"

"We have life, son. And that's more than I can say for the poor souls General Revari and Queen Vivant sent screaming into the sun! I've lived more years than you. I've watched General Revari grow."

Thinking of all the times he'd encountered her made him shudder.

"She's even more ruthless than her father, and that's saying a lot! She ordered me to administer the dose of Ashion over the course of several days so he'd suffer instead of dying instantly."

He could tell Simonius was only half listening to him. He slipped the blade into his pocket. He wasn't worth killing. In the end, his overbearing confidence would contribute to his downfall.

"Trust me, you don't want to die slowly of its poison or be thrown to languish in the Flames of Justice. She did the princesses a favor by giving them a quick death! Even if you're devoid of it, my common sense tells me never to cross her."

"I'm going to bring her son to Platirius, one way or another. He will be the ruler we need—the one we've waited for."

"You're on your own on that one. I haven't waited for any MaleForm to take over Platirius. You haven't thought this through. You need to take a step back."

"I can't afford to do that! I can't risk either of them discovering what I've been doing!"

"You brought it on yourself! You should've kept it zipped! Instead, you indulged in your selfish desires and cut your own throat. You won't receive any help from me!" he said as he stormed out.

He threw the pin at the nearest TranScreen. It didn't matter what Dr. Barrios said—he had no plans of being at Queen Vivant's and General Revari's mercy.

"No one will take my life!" he screamed. "No one!"

"Are you certain of that, Simonius?" asked Queen Vivant.

Whirling around in shock, he saw her standing with the Vivacians and...Dr. Barrios!

"You traitor!"

"The only traitor here is you. And you're a murderer. We found Aja's body in the confinement chamber. You had no right to decide whether she lived or died."

"You would've killed her anyway. Just like you killed all those MaleForms."

"If I were you, I'd worry about my own life. Take him away."

He snarled and tried to fight off the army of WomenForm soldiers as they overpowered him. He was locked away in the dark, screaming at the top of his lungs while they left him alone to contemplate his end.

A fter witnessing Queen Vivant's appointment, she was seething. She'd been demoted to general! She'd sooner resurrect King Dubian than follow orders from her! Opening up her portable TranScreen, she tried to reach Major Legend. She was thoroughly irritated when Simonius's face appeared.

Smoldering with impatience, she glared at him. "What do you want?"

"General Revari. Queen Vivant has imprisoned me!"

The contempt in her face was potent enough to touch.

"What does that have to do with me?"

"They locked me up, but not Major Legend! She's betrayed you. She—she killed your son!"

"You'd better start making sense very quickly or I'll kill you where you stand!"

"I probed her mind when I—when I copulated with her."

She gripped the TranScreen tightly. "*You what?!*"

His voice trembled with fear. "Please listen to me. If I tell you what I know, will you have my life spared?"

Her tongue moistened her lips in anticipation. "Where are you?"

"In the confinement chamber."

Apathetic to his plight, she shrugged. "Then that's where you'll remain. I'll get the truth from her myself."

"But wait—General Revari!"

She cut him off and resent the transmission to Major Legend. She appeared immediately.

"General Revari! By the Heavens, I'm so glad you're safe! Where are you?"

"I'm still on Earth," she said evenly. "I'm more concerned about you. Has Queen Vivant captured you for copulating with Simonius?"

Her face turned gray. "I can explain—"

"I'm more interested in you explaining to me what you know about my son's death. Simonius said you played a part in his murder."

Major Legend's heart raced wildly. "He's lying! It's not true! I never harmed him!"

General Revari scratched a single nail down the screen. "Then what did you do? And what did he see that I don't know? Keep in mind I don't have to be on Platirius to kill you."

"He's alive! Your son didn't die! The InfantForm King Dubian sent into the sun was a sickly one I took from a WomanForm who died. I switched him with your son."

She hadn't realized she was holding her breath. *Could it be true? Had he survived?*

"Where is my son?"

"He's on Earth with you. He knows me as Aunt Legend."

She snarled. "You appointed yourself the authority over *my* son! You knew he was alive and where he's been all this time, and you never told me!"

"I couldn't! I was afraid Queen Vivant would probe my mind at any moment. I couldn't even risk thinking of it. If she knew, she'd kill both of us!"

She kept talking as General Revari fumed, trying to calm her rage. "I've been loyal to you. I saved him so he could one day be reunited with you. It would've happened once you became the sole queen of Platirius."

What does he look like?

She wondered if she'd crossed paths with him on Earth.

"But Queen Vivant and The One stopped it from happening. I would've told you as soon as Earth was absorbed into Platirius. He belongs with you. You deserve to be a MotherForm to him after all this time."

The urge to kill Major Legend nearly consumed her. It would have to wait.

"Where is he, Legend?"

Only after she revealed her son's identity and location did she expel the breath she'd been holding. Her son! *Alive!* She had so many questions.

"What are you going to do? I'm with some of your Revaltians, Gallium, and Dr. Barrios. We still remain loyal to you. We won't work under Queen Vivant!"

Her mind was spinning. A part of her—and Oliver—was *alive*.

"Gallium built a bunker last year. It's still a part of Platirius, regardless of the merger. There's plenty of provisions and water for all of you. Hide in that until I return. I'm going to find my son!"

"We bid you good luck," said Major Legend. "We'll wait for you here."

As she turned to leave, she was caught by a bright, gold blast of light. She never had the chance to open the door.

"It's been hours," said Major Legend. "I told her exactly where to find him. It shouldn't have taken her this long to return to Platirius."

"Check with her son," suggested Gallium. "Maybe she's still playing catch up with him."

She used her TeleScreen to call Dr. Justin Ascencio, the only son of General Revari and Oliver Ascencio.

He saw the call appear on his dashboard and quickly pulled over to answer.

"Hey, Aunt Legend. What's up?"

"Hi Justin. I need to ask an important question. Has your mother visited you?"

Distracted, he paused to notice a gorgeous woman leaving a coffee shop. "My mother?" he asked, watching the woman enter her car. "I just dropped her off at home."

"No, not her. I'm asking about your birth mother."

He paused. "No, I haven't seen her, but why would I? Has something happened?"

She sighed. "Yes, a lot has happened. Remember I told you this day would come."

He disconnected the speakerphone and turned off the engine. "What's going on?"

"Something is wrong! I spoke with her hours ago. She should've contacted you by now."

He expelled a long breath. "Maybe she doesn't want to see me. Maybe the thought of finally accepting responsibility for her kid cramps her style."

"Oh no. Never believe that! She only recently learned you're alive. Nothing would ever change her mind about loving you."

"Well...then maybe you're right. Maybe something bad happened to her. People prey on the elderly all the time."

Her mouth dropped while Gallium chuckled.

"Justin...How old do you think your mother is?"

He shrugged. "I don't know. Late sixties?"

Gallium laughed harder.

"How old do I look?" she asked pointedly.

She waited for him to assess her. "Hmm. Late twenties?"

"I am five million years old. And so is your mother."

His eyebrows raised. "If that's true, then how are you still alive? Even for Aliens, you should be hunched over like candy canes."

Dr. Barrios and Gallium looked at each other and nearly fell over laughing. Major Legend and Justin ignored them.

"And I thought she was a queen and you were the general?"

She bit her lip. "It's a long story."

"Maybe we should bring him here?" said Dr. Barrios.

She stared at him. "To Platirius? With Queen Vivant tracking us like a blood-sniffing bounty hunter?"

"I don't think she'll hurt the boy," said Gallium. "In fact, he may be the key to all of us getting off Platirius and finding her."

"He might be correct in his assumption," said Dr. Barrios. "Queen Vivant is also responsible for breaking up her family. I doubt she'd be so callous to try and hurt the boy."

"You can stop calling me a boy. I'm a grown man," said Justin curtly. "And a physician like you."

"I see he takes after his mother," muttered Dr. Barrios.

Gallium entered data into his TeleScreen. "Her last coordinates were closer to Platirius than Earth. Then they drifted off in another direction—on the other side of the galaxy. That means she's no longer on Earth. We have a better chance of searching closer to home than there."

"I can bring you here to help us find your mother if you'd like," said Major Legend.

"Yeah, I'll come. I've been waiting a long time to meet her."

Before he could blink, he was standing in front of Major Legend, Gallium, Dr. Barrios, and dozens of the most beautiful women he'd seen in his entire life. They were scantily clad in red armor, sheer leggings, and high-heeled boots.

"Is this Heaven?" he asked.

"This is Platirius," said Major Legend.

"I'm aware," he retorted. "I was making a joke."

"Never joke about the realm of The One," she told him.

"Ouch," he said, looking over the grim faces. "Tough crowd."

"Major Legend! By order of Queen Vivant, you and everyone under there come out or we'll blow you out!"

"Who in the world is that?" asked Justin.

"The insufferable General Lyric," said Gallium. "I despise her."

"We all do," said Major Legend. "They've found us. We have no choice but to go to them. Stay behind me, Justin."

As they filed out of the bunker, Queen Vivant's gaze was instantly drawn to Justin.

General Lyric raised her sword. "A Human! Halt!"

"If you touch him, I'll kill you!" declared Major Legend, unsheathing her sword. She moved him closer behind her.

"Take him!" ordered General Lyric.

As the Vivacians moved in to capture him, Platirius rumbled and split open. Buried under the platinum soil was an ancient BrainStaff. It rose slowly from the ground, hovering before it gained speed, and flew toward him.

Lifting his hand swiftly, it sprang to his grasp with a hard *thuck*. Suddenly, he felt more robust, more powerful than he ever had in his life.

Captain Kourtney gasped. "He's a Platirian! How can this be?"

Queen Vivant looked as if she'd seen a ghost. In fact, she had. The Human-MaleForm was holding King Dubian's BrainStaff, and with it, was absorbing all the knowledge of Platirius. In seconds, his mind processed memories of all the past MaleForm rulers of Platirius as he inherited their knowledge and strength—from King Dubian to the first king to absorb a planet into its realm.

He now knew who his mother was and...the identity of the woman who stood before him. King Dubian's BrainStaff showed him everything that had transpired on Platirius for millions of years—including the torture and murder of his father, grandparents, and aunt. Rage surged within him as he stared at Queen Vivant.

"I should cut off your head and take this planet," he told her.

Immediately, the Vivacians surrounded their queen, preparing for an attack. He slowly circled his neck, sending sharp cracking sounds ringing into the night.

"Vivacians, stand down," she ordered.

Immediately, they followed her command. His mouth curled into a sly smile.

"You're not as dumb as you look." His voice deepened under the power of the spirits of dozens of kings. "You're realizing I've just inherited the strength of every king who's ever ruled Platirius. I could wipe out your army without blinking."

She raised her BrainStaff. "I suppose you'll try. But never think I'll allow a MaleForm to rule Platirius."

"I don't want your stupid planet," he said. "What I want is to find my mother."

He pointed the BrainStaff at her and said, "And you're going to help us find her. If you don't, I will raze Platirius to the ground and leave your people in ashes. You don't want to have more innocent blood on your hands than you already have, do you?"

He means his father. "I don't wish to harm you," she told him.

"It's a little too late to start playing the role of a loving aunt. You didn't think I was good enough to live here as an infant, and you still feel that way. You didn't think twice before destroying my family. How ironic is it to lose your daughters. In the end, you got what you deserved."

Dr. Barrios and Gallium stared at him in amazement. They'd never heard a MaleForm speak to her that way. Never.

"It's true," she admitted. "I had a hand in the destruction of my sister's family. The past will always aggrieve me, but I can't change it. You say she's missing?"

"Yes, and after you point us in the right direction, we're leaving Platirius to find her. Not you, specifically. I doubt my mother wants to see you after you stole the planet she rightfully restored."

"I stole nothing. I was appointed to lead Platirius by The One. While it's true she conquered Earth through the acquisition of souls—"

"As all other rulers of Platirius have done long before Platirius existed—" he interrupted.

"—she interfered in the war between Heaven and Hell. That could not be overlooked," she finished. "And she was subsequently denied the right to rule Platirius and demoted to general."

He bristled. "To serve Platirius under your authority! You're still giving her the scraps even when she's earned the head seat at the table! I've never met her, but I know she won't serve under you. Where does that leave her? She's right back where she started—the outsider looking in on the planet she helped build! It isn't fair to her!"

"I don't want to fight with you. Let us work together to search for her. I'd like to prepare my army to search for her—"

His cold stare was reminiscent of her father's. "I don't need you. I, along with everyone who's been loyal to her, will search for her. And mind you, as long as I'm here, they're under my protection. Just point me in the right direction."

Major Legend breathed a sigh of relief and smirked at General Lyric.

Queen Vivant stared pityingly at him. "You don't make the rules here. I do."

Her eyes slid to Major Legend. "The ones cowering behind you have broken the laws of Platirius and won't escape judgment. I'm willing to enter a temporary truce with you until we find her. But I assure you, I intend to see Major Legend and any other Revaltian who copulated with Simonius punished."

She ignored the indignant whispers of some of the Revaltians. Had General Revari not been missing, they knew she would've quickly carried out their punishment. Still, none of them wanted to test the limits of her patience.

"If you want to battle with me for their sake, you are welcome to. However, that would be time better spent finding my sister."

"I'll cross that bridge when it's time. You're not allowed to have sex here? No wonder most of the women act so weird. That'd be the first rule I'd change as king."

"Spoken like a true MaleForm," said Queen Vivant.

"Better than acting like an arrogant prude," he retorted.

She raised an eyebrow. "Come with me."

Leading the group into her meeting chamber with the Vivacians following in tow, she pulled up her last known coordinates. "I'll have to use her *nued* points to find her. I doubt you'd want to see your mother unclothed. Please close your eyes."

Out of respect for General Revari, everyone turned their backs on the TranScreen as she entered data into the highly advanced search engine. Moments later, she stared at the screen, unable to believe what she saw.

"She's on Kikhani!"

"What is that and where is it?" asked Justin.

"The Kikhanians are the sworn enemies of Platirius," said Major Legend. "They've stolen her!"

"Then we're going to Kikhani to get her back!" he said.

"The Kikhanians are powerful Beings," said Queen Vivant. "Their armies are advanced and equipped with weapons you've never encountered. You'll need our help to rescue her."

"I hate to admit it, but she's right." said Major Legend.

"And what happens when we find my mother?" he asked. "You heard her say she'll punish you and the other women!"

"We're WomenForms, not women," said a Vivacian soldier.

"What's the difference? All of you are acting as if you're too good to get on your knees for men."

Rounds of shocked gasps and indignant cries rang out as Gallium and Dr. Barrios kept expressionless faces. They weren't going to give Queen Vivant an excuse to kill them when she finally delved out punishment.

Queen Vivant met General Lyric's eyes. *This is why MaleForms must never rule Platirius.*

"Why?" asked Prince Justin. "Because we tell the truth?"

Startled, she looked at him.

He cocked his head. "Oh, you didn't know one of my newly inherited powers was mind reading? Sorry about that, Queen Vivant."

He emphasized *queen* with just enough disrespect to enrage her, but she held her temper in check. He was a crude reincarnation of King Anemi, his great-grandfather. She was trying hard not to loathe him, but it wasn't easy.

"I'm not asking for nor do I need your permission to find my sister. Vivacians, make preparations to go to Kikhani. We'll leave in the morning."

Spinning on her heel, she left the unwanted guests standing in her meeting chamber.

"Yes, Queen Vivant," said General Lyric. Turning to peruse him, she said, "I'll escort you to your quarters, Prince Justin. MaleForms don't bunk with WomenForms. I'll have the dining staff prepare your meals and bring them to you. We don't eat with them either."

In the bunker, he'd been put off by her low, gravely voice, but hadn't expected her to be so beautiful. "You're much too pretty to be a general. Have you ever been kissed? Never mind. If you knew how, you wouldn't be so uptight. When this is over, I'd like to teach you if you ask nicely."

He laughed at the outraged expressions on every WomanForm's face except the ones who knew how copulation felt. She stared him down. He was testing her. He was half-royal, and she, a commoner. Although he wasn't technically a ruler, she was powerless to defend herself against his bold proposition.

"I see you waited until you were out of the queen's earshot to spew such foulness."

He shook his head. "I'm not afraid of her. I meant no disrespect, but seeing you walk around with so much...repressed energy is a shame. You're a beautiful woman. There's more to life than taking orders and threatening to kill people, you know."

She wanted to punch him in the throat. Giving a full Platirian salute, she said, "Follow me please, Prince Justin."

How many of them hate men? he wondered.

He wanted to meet Simonius. Maybe he'd give him pointers on how he'd melted some of these walking igloos.

Queen Vivant had no intention of allowing them to meet. While the MaleForms and the rest of the Revaltians ate a late supper, he was hauled from the confinement chamber and packed tightly into a death vessel.

He strained against the steel straps that held him down. "I've been loyal to Platirius! You have no right to do this!"

"You don't know the meaning of loyalty. Be grateful I'm giving you a quick death instead of throwing you into the Flames of Justice. I have every right to ship you off my planet. General Revari advocated for your life to be spared, and how did you repay her?"

"Major Legend forced herself on me," he lied. "I couldn't say no!"

"Do you realize now that I'm better, I have the power to scan your mind? I've seen every treacherous act you committed. You've earned your fate." Turning to General Lyric, she said, "Send him off."

Every Platirian was in attendance to watch him be sent into the sun. As the last of his screams faded into Space, everyone agreed he wouldn't be missed.

Major Legend was pleased when she spied the craft carrying him fly off Platirius. She never should've copulated with him, but the urges had threatened to overwhelm her. Gallium's *Quinite*—a drug he'd invented for suppressing sexual urges—was good for suppressing the urges, but once General Revari became queen, she appointed her.

The never-ending responsibility of overseeing nearly three thousand soldiers replaced taking care of herself. She rarely had time to eat or get adequate sleep. After awhile, she'd stopped taking the *Quinite*.

She hoped all the years she'd been loyal to General Revari would save her life. She didn't respect or trust Queen Vivant. Although she'd acted as if Prince Justin's presence had made a difference in her not being sent off into the sun with Simonius, she knew better.

Clearly, Queen Vivant felt guilty for depriving General Revari of the opportunity to be a MotherForm, but that didn't mean she'd allow him to sway her from killing her and the rest of the Revaltians. Major Legend didn't think it was wise for her to enter into a battle with him.

He possessed the strength and knowledge of all the former kings of Platirius. That wasn't to be taken lightly. Second, General Revari would never forgive her for hurting her son if she managed to win against him.

Finally, although she loved him as a nephew, he was half-MaleForm. It was dangerous to allow a MaleForm to rule Platirius—especially one from a long lineage of oppressive, misogynistic kings.

She had remained close to him as he grew up on Earth. When he was old enough to understand, she'd informed him of who he was and where he came from. He'd grown to be a son his mother would've been proud of.

His temperament was more like his Human father's than his mother's. He was shy, quiet, and almost meek. However, once he'd inherited the power of his ancestors, his personality changed drastically. Now he was just as crude and disrespectful to WomenForms as they had been.

She was all for a reunion between him and General Revari, but she'd never support him taking the throne. It was a fine line she walked between him and Queen Vivant. She had to trust their friendship would save her from both if she found herself on his bad side.

In her heart, she felt her friend was still alive. She looked up at the stars. "Don't worry, General Revari. We're coming to bring you home."

After breakfast, Queen Vivant, the Vivacians, Major Legend, the Revaltians, and Prince Justin boarded the expansive WarCraft. Gallium and Dr. Barrios stayed behind, locked away in the confinement chamber.

Queen Vivant didn't trust them to be free on Platirius until she returned. She suspected Prince Justin's powers would give them an advantage against the all-WomenForm army of Kikhani, since their planet was younger than Platirius and had fewer rulers over the years.

She stood before the group, preparing them for what may be the last fight of their lives.

"It's been a thousand years since Platirius went to war with Kikhani. I wish I could tell you all of us will return home, but that's not the case. The Kikhanians have no honor. They don't fight fairly and show no mercy to their enemies."

All eyes were on her. Every soldier understood the importance of the upcoming battle.

"Our mission is to go in and rescue General Revari. I'm speaking to all WomenForms when I say we are the greatest force in the galaxy, and we are one army now."

Sheila and Angela, General Revari's best soldiers, side-eyed each other. They had craftily hidden their thoughts from her. The Revaltians heard her, but in their eyes, General Revari was still their leader.

They were ready to join forces with the Vivacians to rescue her, but swearing allegiance to Queen Vivant was out of the question. The Surveyors' vision had been accurate—both armies would remain loyal to their commanders until death.

"We are a single unit of Platirians prepared to fight and die to free her. There cannot and will not be any bickering or fighting among us. The stakes are too high. The Kikhanians fight and breathe as a united force. It's their best military tactic. If we are to survive, we must duplicate it."

She looked around at them and asked, "Are you ready?"

A loud roar sounded in the WarCraft. Every Platirian was ready to face and defeat their enemy.

"General Lyric," she commanded. "Drop the protective shield."

She followed her queen's order and a beautiful golden planet appeared in the distance. Queen Vivant surveyed her army once more, proud to lead them into battle. Silently, she prayed to The One for guidance as they floated toward a calamitous colony, unaware if or when they'd return to Platirius.

Epilogue

General Lyric noticed him watching her and tried her best to ignore him. She was grateful they didn't eat together. She didn't know what she'd do if he tried to get to know her more intimately.

Prince Justin thought she hated MaleForms, but that wasn't true. Growing up with the knowledge that she'd never be viewed as anything more than a source of pleasure for them made her eschew forming platonic bonds with them.

While in General Kron's army, her fellow MaleForm soldiers had made it clear she'd never be their equal. She wasn't happy when he died, but she knew there was no way she would've been promoted had he lived.

As the leader of Platirius's army, he'd made it difficult for WomenForms to achieve advancement. Although he appeared warm and loving towards Princess Vivant, he extended no such sentiments to other WomenForms.

Except for Princess Revari, she, Private Legend, and others who joined under his leadership were treated abhorrently by the other MaleForms. Hoping their intolerance would force them to quit, he did nothing to stop it.

At first, she'd tried to befriend Private Legend, but she wanted nothing to do with her. Eventually, she became friends with the two remaining WomenForm soldiers. After they died in battle, she was alone.

When Queen Vivant succeeded to the throne, she saw potential in her. Were it not for her, General Lyric didn't know how her life would've turned out. She was grateful for the sisterhood she'd found in the Vivacians.

Now, after meeting Prince Justin, she struggled to fight the conflicting feelings burgeoning within her. How had he known she'd never been kissed? She shook her head as if to rid her mind of such thoughts.

Even if he hadn't been a royal, the penalty for copulating with a MaleForm was death. He wasn't worth risking her life and career for. She had to continue ignoring him until he returned to Earth. She'd rather it be sooner than later.

Her cool façade didn't fool Justin. He was good-looking, charming, and very attuned to his effect on women—on and off Earth. He'd noticed more than a few of the Alien women kept darting secret glances his way when they thought Queen Vivant wasn't looking—including General Lyric.

He suspected she was just as intrigued by him as he was by her. He didn't know how things would pan out or if he'd make it out of Space alive, but he planned to learn everything about her once his mother was safe. A star streaked across Space, illuminated by the encompassing darkness.

He smiled. *Hello Fate.*

Platirius: Kikhani vs Platirius

General Revari silently assessed her. "I don't think you have room to talk about what happens between fathers and unwanted daughters. Mine hated me, but at least he wanted me to live on Platirius. Your father left because," her voice lowered to a whisper, "he could no longer stand the sight of you and your weak-minded mother."

She paused before continuing. "You allowed him to walk out on you. It would've been best if you used that blade to cut his neck open. It might've saved your mother's honor."

Queen Aiki looked at her sharply. She stood still for a moment, reflecting on her words. Finally, she cocked her head. "Don't go anywhere. I'll return shortly."

In less than ten minutes, she returned with two trays loaded with half of a roast chicken, herbed dressing, sweet potatoes swimming in honey and butter, and thick slices of apple pie a la mode.

She used her powers to release her from the invisible bands around her arms and ankles. Brimming with excitement, she looked at the spread laid before them. "Come! Eat with me."

General Revari rubbed her sore arms, looking over the food warily.

"I didn't poison it!" She took a bite of food from both trays. "See?" Come, come, sit down! I don't like cold food."

Sore from hanging in a single position for hours, she gently eased her body down to sit at the table. Like a small ChildForm, Queen Aiki clapped her hands in delight.

"Isn't this nice? The lights. The ambiance. Dinner is best served in my home, but I don't trust you, General Revari. If you killed your own family, who knows what you'd do to me."

General Revari's mouth curled slightly. "Touche," she said.

They ate silently for a moment before General Revari caught her staring pensively at her.

"Yes?"

"I'm usually not accommodating to guests, but you've been given an excellent meal. Now, I want you to do something for me."

General Revari looked around at the tacky gold decorations before settling her eyes on her again. She was living proof being born into royalty didn't account for good taste.

"I'm not surprised. If I were of no use to you, I would've died sooner than later."

The queen of Kikhani simply smiled. General Revari sat back in the chair, pressing her fingers together as she imagined a dozen ways to kill her.

The nerve of Queen Aiki interrupting her plans just as she was headed to find her son. Her timing was as lousy as her taste in decorating. If she'd wanted a confrontation, she'd had years to face her. She tried to scan her mind but it was no use. Her mind was too discombobulated to discern why she'd been brought to Kikhani.

"What do you want from me?" she asked finally.

Queen Aiki's gold eyes roamed over her. "Tell me how to kill my father."

D.L.'s Note

Dear Reader,

Congratulations on your second voyage to Platirius! What did you like most about the story? How do you feel now that you've uncovered Queen Revari's past? I was inspired to continue developing her truth from a nature vs nurture perspective. How many people are walking around with unresolved pain?

As for Queen Vivant, self-reflection was inevitable for her to grow and become better for herself and her fellow Platirians. Platirius: The Rise of Reve is about living with the consequences of our actions. At times, we don't realize what we do and say causes a ripple effect in the lives of others. As you continue reading about the Platirians, I hope you become committed to confronting things we sometimes are reluctant to face.

Stay tuned for the third installment, Platirius: Kikhani vs Platirius! I'm excited to get it into your hands. Happy reading and thank you for your continued support!

xoxo D.L. Hannah

Author Bio

D.L. Hannah was born in Youngstown, Ohio. She is a writer, entrepreneur, and host of the Amerisogyny podcast. She is a Psi Chi and Alpha Kappa Delta member and earned a Bachelor of Arts degree in Clinical-Community Psychology from Walsh University. For over twenty years, she has been a strong advocate for children diagnosed with Autism. She now lives in North Carolina with her family.

Join D.L.'s VIP List

https://www.dlhannah.com

Also by D.L. Hannah